D1072040

Senior Nurse
A KATHY MARTIN STORY

by JOSEPHINE JAMES

illustrated by KENNETH ROSSI

GOLDEN PRESS · NEW YORK

TABLE OF CONTENTS

CHAPTER I

Summer's End

"Thank you, Doctor," Kathy murmured. *"But I'm sure any nurse would have done as well."*

The doctor did not answer—hardly a surprising fact, for no doctor was there. Nor any hospital corridor, or sterile operating room. Only a fat and lazy cloud inching along a lazy summer sky, and the heavily gnarled, gray trunk of an apple tree too old to be part of the orchard. The *babuchka* tree, Big Nick Martin always called it— the grandmother tree, watching over young saplings and young Martins alike. Kathy herself had cared for innumerable sick dolls among the roots of the old tree. Here she had dreamed of becoming a nurse; or, more often, had daydreamed of *being* a nurse without having to bother with the unknowns of learning how.

"Thank you, Doctor. Any nurse would have done the same." That was an old favorite among the daydreams. In an operating room, on board a ship in a raging storm, on the steps of the Taj Mahal in India or the Parthenon in Greece . . . wherever Kathy's imagination strayed, an R.N. appeared—tall, brown-haired and amazingly skill-

ful—modestly accepting the praise that was, of course, her due. Here, too, Clara Barton had come alive; and Florence Nightingale, "the Lady of the Lamp"; and Louisa May Alcott, nursing back to health the heroes of the Civil War.

Two years ago, Kathy Martin, R.N.—the nurse in world-wide demand—had faded from the steps of the Taj Mahal and ceased to roam the Seven Seas. In her place, Kathy Martin, student nurse at San Tomás Hospital, had made beds, given enemas, taken temperatures, learned the languages of cells and muscles, instruments and equipment, drugs and diseases. There had been no glamor to offset aching feet, tired eyes, and the drudgery that was part of a student nurse's life. Nevertheless, Kathy had found the reality of becoming a nurse even better than the dreams.

Kathy stretched out luxuriously in the long grass.

Tomorrow senior year would begin. There were only a few more hours left of vacation. A sudden impulse had brought her down to the old tree—leaving her packing unfinished, her dress still to be pressed for the last summer date with Steve Kovak.

Since Steve had been a part of her life, daydream romances with daydream doctors had seemed unnecessary. Her mind drifted back pleasantly over the past four weeks. She and Steve had had more time together than ever before. Picnics, dancing, swimming, exploring Corralitos Creek all the way up the canyon. Steve had helped with the farming, too, this summer. Kathy's father even had him driving the tractor on one of his days off from his fire-fighting job. That was an honor indeed.

Steve was competent in everything he did. A little too competent, Kathy sometimes thought. Maybe that was why she drifted off into another daydream . . . Kathy Martin, R.N., standing by a hospital bed, smiling down at a good-looking young man about to be discharged after a remarkable recovery.

"I never would have made it except for you, Kathy. The doctor told me, but I knew it already . . . and Kathy, you know, don't you, how much I need you and . . ."

A combination of sounds behind her startled Kathy out of her daydream.

"Johnny Martin, what on earth are you doing?"

Not that Kathy could fail to see—and hear—what Johnny was doing. The latest family disaster had been that Cousin Marie Nicholas had given Johnny an accordion for his seventh birthday. He had managed to master just part of one song, but he moved the bellows in and out with fantastic enthusiasm. Armed with the instrument, he bore down on Kathy. His dog, Spot, followed behind, barking an off-beat accompaniment. The combo was completed by Quacky, the newest pet, protesting as loud as a duck could at the indignity of being pulled along on a leash.

"We're having a parade! Can't you see?"

"Well, you'd better let poor Quacky go, or I'll have to treat her for pharyngolaryngitis."

"You will?" Johnny was impressed. Evidently Quacky was impressed also, because with a flash of ingenuity and a snakelike twist of her neck she freed herself from the leash and fled to the pond, squawking triumphantly.

"I guess she don't like accordion music," Johnny said. "Oh, well, me and Spot—I mean, I and Spot—can be a parade. Want to hear me do *Happy Birthday*, Kath? Part of it, I mean? Do you?"

"Not now, Johnny, please . . ."

"Okay. I'll play it when Steve gets here. I wish he'd come in his fire engine—Quacky never saw Steve standing on that step with the sirens going *whr-r-r* . . . Oh, that reminds me. Mama said Steve called from the firehouse—and he got off early and he'll be here for supper and we should get some corn and hurry up."

"Oh, Johnny!" Kathy glanced at her wrist watch and scrambled to her feet. Four-thirty! Somehow the afternoon had slipped away. Packing not done. Dress not pressed. And Steve coming in twenty minutes!

"Look, Johnny, you can't pick corn with your accordion on. Go put it away and I'll get the corn. And listen, tell Mama to please plug the iron in. Can you remember that? Please now, don't start talking about three other things."

"What three other things?"

"*No* three other things. Just ask Mama to plug in the

iron so it will be hot when I get back to the house."

"But I still don't see what three other things—"

"Oh, go ahead, Johnny, *please!*" Kathy ran along the hillside to the truck garden and moved down the rows of corn, watching for the stalks where the cornsilk was just starting to turn brown. She loaded her arms with a dozen ripe ears. Five minutes to press her dress, ten minutes to change . . . if Johnny didn't forget about the iron.

"Say, Kath, would an ear of corn be good for pharry— that thing you said Quacky might get?"

Johnny's round face appeared between two corn stalks. A gesture of sheer exasperation made Kathy drop the armload of corn. Quacky moved in with a suspiciously healthy chortle and went to work on the nearest ear.

"Johnny, didn't I tell you—"

Kathy's explosion was cut off as a deep voice, full of suppressed amusement, said gravely, "Don't you think that's a little too much corn for one duck to consume, Nurse Martin?"

"Steve!" Blushing furiously, Kathy bent down and began to pick up the corn.

Steve Kovak walked down from the little knoll above the corn patch. "See you up at the house, Johnny," he said firmly. "And your feathered friend, too!"

Johnny fled, glad of the interruption.

"Here, Kathy, let me take the corn. Do you know you look pretty when you're mad?"

Steve reached out, and Kathy suddenly found herself—corn and all—imprisoned in a quick embrace. Exasperation and embarrassment slipped away as Kathy rested her head for an instant on Steve's shoulder.

"You could pass for Miss California Harvest," Steve said as he took the last ear of corn. "Complete with cornsilk on your shirt and a crown of hayseed—or is that wild wheat? What have you been doing—gathering seed to smuggle back to San Tomás?"

"Caught with the goods!" Kathy ran her hand hastily through her short brown curls. "Evidence of idle hours, Your Honor. I spent the whole afternoon under my favorite tree, doing absolutely nothing."

The magic light of late afternoon swept over the hillside. Steve and Kathy paused halfway up to the house, caught by the sudden brightness of the orchard. Beyond the orchard, the foothills climbing to the coastal mountains had taken on amazing hues of blue and gray, crimson and purple.

Kathy wished suddenly that the San Tomás Hospital could be transported seventy-five miles south into the Appleton hills.

"Hey, down there!" Young Nick's voice came from the barbecue pit behind the house. "Are you two planting that corn, or just waiting for it to get ripe?"

"Brothers!" Kathy laughed affectionately. Nick, at eighteen, had suddenly taken on the look of a man. Whether he would take the scholarship offered him at agricultural school, or stay on the ranch and learn to be an orchardist the hard way, was still to be decided.

In two minutes the ears of corn—husks and all—were resting on hot coals. Delighted at the impromptu picnic, Kathy flew to the house to lend her mother a hand.

Ella Martin looked up from the ironing board. Her round, pleasant face was flushed with the heat. Kathy felt a twinge of guilt as her mother pressed out the last folds of the full-skirted summer dress.

"I'm sorry, Mom—"

"Special treatment for your last vacation day," Ella Martin said cheerfully. "Supper's all set. I just have to take the salad down—and get a few herbs on the way." Ella Martin never managed to serve a meal without "a few herbs" from her garden. "Papa's cleaning up, and he'll be down to superintend the steak."

"Steak! A real feast!"

"Steve brought the steak. He didn't think your father would want to spare you for supper at Loma Linda on your last night home."

"Quite right." Big Nick Martin came into the kitchen, seeming, as always, to fill the whole room.

"Can Quacky come to supper?" Johnny, minus the accordion, poked his head in through the back door.

"I suppose so," Mrs. Martin laughed. "When I think that we planned on a duck dinner this summer!"

"But she keeps all the snails off the flowers, Mama. and lays eggs and—"

"And manages to keep reasonably clean." Mr. Martin frowned down at his small son. "Which is more than I can say for you, young man. Get washed. With speed!"

"I'll supervise neck and ears," Kathy said, "and be down as soon as I change. Thanks a million, Mom." She leaned over to give her mother a quick kiss as she picked up the dress. "A picnic supper . . . with corn *and* steak. And dancing with Steve at Loma Linda—this is one vacation that's really going to end with a bang!"

CHAPTER II

Kelley's Groceries

The Merriweather house, used as the Senior Residence for the School of Nursing, had once been a San Tomás showplace. Now the bay windows and curlicue ornaments hid behind shrubs and evergreens, as if they were a little ashamed of their old-fashioned look. Here and there, above the tops of the trees, pointed turrets peered down disapprovingly at the antics of each new generation of students. The endless layers of paint gave the house a faded and wrinkled appearance curiously like that of its present owner, Miss Althea Merriweather.

Miss Merriweather had continued to live in one wing of her house even after she had leased it to the Nursing School. She was as much part of the place as the New England lilac bushes that flourished among the palms and geraniums of the California landscape. Through the dry and dusty August days, Miss Merriweather watered her lilacs. She was out with the hose when Kathy drove up in the pickup truck.

Young Nick, at the wheel, saw the look of surprise on Miss Merriweather's face.

"Guess she's not used to guests driving up to her door in such style," he said dryly.

The pickup was covered with a gray film of dust. The back was piled high with things Kathy thought she and her roommate, Kelley Jones, might need. Johnny was riding on top of the load with Quacky, his duck, squeezed tight in his arms.

"Hey, Kathy! Look at that hose squirting up to the second story! I'm thirsty. Can I ask the funny little old lady for a drink of water for me and Quacky?"

Nick scowled. "Keep your voice down, Johnny! Do you want to get Kathy in Dutch before school begins?"

Kathy smoothed her wind-blown brown curls, unfolded her long legs and climbed down to help unload her belongings.

"Nick's right, Johnny," she said. "You must be careful of other people's feelings. It doesn't matter this time, though. Miss Merriweather's stone-deaf."

"What's stone-deaf?" Johnny asked. "You mean she can't hear any more than a rock?"

"That's about it," Kathy laughed.

"Anyway, do you think she'd let me have a squirt of water from the hose? Quacky wants some water, too."

"The duck stays in the pickup," Kathy said sternly. "We'll bring Quacky some water in a pan, and I'll give you a nice cold drink when we get up to my room. See the bay window with the little balcony? That's where I'm going to live."

Nick counted the suitcases and boxes to be carried up to the third-floor room in the turret and groaned.

"Well, let's get it over with," he said.

"I'd better say hello to Miss Merriweather first," Kathy said. "After all, she's our house mother."

"What's the use of saying hello if she can't hear you?" Johnny objected.

"She reads lips," Kathy said, and left Johnny to figure that one out for himself.

"Stop staring, Johnny, and pick up that bag of corn."

When Kathy came back, Nick had a suitcase in each hand, a tennis racket under one arm and a framed picture of himself taken at his high-school graduation under the other. Kathy gathered up a remaining suitcase, a potted plant and a basket filled with jars of jelly. "Our room is only two flights up," she said cheerfully.

Linda Garfield opened the front door—a disheveled but beaming Linda. Her arms were loaded with bags of beans and boxes of rice. A few grains of rice leaked out as she shifted her burden.

"Kathy! Isn't this super? Just like setting up house-keeping! But I can't understand why Kelley brought things that take so long to cook."

Linda looked a little embarrassed at the sight of Kathy's tall, good-looking and almost grown-up brother.

"I'm just a mess," she said, "and I know my face is dirty. I'll just put these groceries in the kitchen and help you carry your things upstairs."

"I'm thirsty," Johnny began.

A howl from above startled him so that he dropped the corn. It was Kelley's anguished voice. "My mosaics! Linda, come back with my beans and rice!"

"Oh, dear!" Linda looked up the stair well in dismay. "I was just trying to help Kelley get the room straight before you came," she explained. "Do you suppose they make pictures out of beans and rice in Mexico? I'd better take this stuff upstairs again."

Kelley Jones had spent the summer vacation studying ancient art at the University of Vera Cruz in Mexico. She had come back inspired with the idea of creating mosaics from pinto beans, navy beans, rice and corn. Her third-floor room, which Kathy was to share, bore the appearance of an art gallery, a studio and the home of a pack rat. Kathy's belongings, which she and Nick dumped inside the door, did not improve matters. But Kathy looked at the chaos in deep contentment.

"Senior year is going to be wonderful," she said. "I feel it in my bones. Look, Nick, we've got a balcony! And a view of Mount Hamilton!"

"What you girls need is a derrick." Nick rubbed his tired arms, unimpressed. "Or a ski lift. Give Johnny his drink of water and let me get back to my nice quiet job of picking apples."

"Poor Nick. But it's not all madhouse," Linda said. "Come see our room. Gail and I came yesterday. We're beautifully settled."

Kathy looked around in surprise. "Is Gail here?"

"In a way," Kelley answered.

"Come on, I'll show you," Linda said.

They trooped across the hall, and Linda flung open the door. All was serene: curtains and pictures hung, books neatly lined up on a shelf. On a studio couch lay Gail Henderson, in slacks and a bright red shirt. Usually lively and alert, she was studying the ceiling. An unopened detective story had slipped out of her hands to the floor. She raised up on one elbow, turned dreamy eyes in their direction and waved as if half-asleep.

"Behold, Cleopatra on her barge," Kelley announced, "composing sonnets to Mark Antony."

Gently, Linda closed the door. "Not Mark Antony—the name is Christopher Matthews," she said.

"Come on, Johnny," Nick muttered. "Let's get out of here. These girls are nuts."

"But I'm thirsty. So's Quacky," Johnny said.

"I'll buy you both a soda pop on the way home," Nick answered from halfway down the stairs.

"Wait, Nick, till Johnny gets his drink, and a pan of water for Quacky! And thanks—for everything," Kathy called after him. "And, Nick, we're not always crazy. You wouldn't think so if you saw us in uniform tomorrow!"

CHAPTER III

Something New

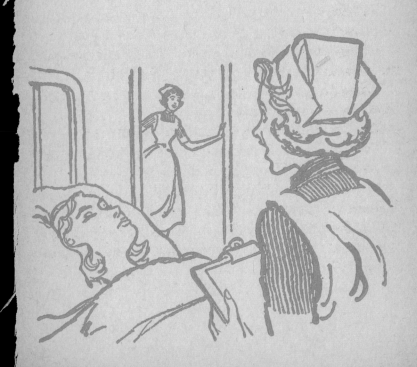

"One time, when I was about fourteen years old," Linda said, "I ran the length of the high-school gym dribbling a basketball. I ran very fast and nobody intercepted me. There I was with the ball and up there was the basket. I tossed the ball. *Plonk!* Right into the basket."

Jenny Ramirez leaned across the table, interested and surprised. "You never told us you played basketball in high school, Linda."

"That was the last time." Linda giggled nervously and pushed a curl under her cap. "And it was the only time I ever made a basket. It—it counted two points for the other team. I had gotten turned around and—"

"How can a girl be so loquacious at six o'clock in the morning—and on a cup of cocoa?" Kelley sighed as she gloomily nursed her second cup of coffee.

Kathy came to Linda's defense. "It's not loquaciousness, it's the jitters at beginning something new."

"What's new about AM shift at San Tomás Hospital, for heaven's sake?" Kelley looked defiantly up and down the long, familiar table by the cafeteria window. "Just

24

because we're Seniors won't make a bit of difference on the bedpan parade."

"But there *is* something new," Linda answered, refusing for once to wilt under Kelley's scoffing. "Not one of us has ever been a team leader before."

Team leadership was the responsibility that loomed before them all. As team leaders they would have not only their own duties but the responsibility of supervising the Junior nurses and the aides in their group. There'd be no experienced R.N. to direct or advise them —except, of course, for the head nurse in charge of the whole floor. The welfare of half a dozen patients would depend on the team leader. A mistake made by any member of the team would be the leader's mistake.

Soberly and silently the four girls finished their breakfast and filed into the elevator that would take them to their first Senior duties.

"Second West for me," Kathy said. The surgical-medical ward was her old stamping ground. It felt good to be back, to see rosy-cheeked Mrs. Rice bent over her paper work at the Nurses' Station.

"You're early, Martin," Mrs. Rice said approvingly. "Sit down and we'll go over your charts and your team list. You'll have Cranshaw for your Junior nurse, Tillie Anderson and Mrs. Stein for aides."

Kathy checked off each name in her mind. Mary Cranshaw had been Kelley's Little Sister last year. She was president of the Junior class, capable and reliable. Having Mary on her team gave Kathy a feeling of renewed confidence. On the other hand, Tillie Anderson might be a trial. She had come to work at the hospital in June, just out of high school. She was young and brash and still had a lot to learn. Mrs. Stein's name didn't ring a bell.

"Mrs. Stein has just come down to us from Surgery," the nurse-in-charge said.

Then Kathy remembered the odd-looking aide in the sterilizing room of the surgical wing. "The Rabbit," Gail used to call her, insisting that her mop of red hair was a wig to cover rabbit ears. When Mrs. Stein passed out the dressing and instrument trays, she had a way of looking through and around you, with frightened eyes, quite like a rabbit about to dart into the shrubbery. Kathy couldn't imagine, couldn't picture, this silent, timid aide taking care of a patient.

Mrs. Rice glanced at the clock. "It's almost time for your team conference," she was saying. "We'll just run through the charts."

So the first day began. The duties promised to be comparatively simple. None of the patients was on the DI list—there were none, that is, who were dangerously ill. Two appendectomies were making normal recoveries. An old man with a stroke had his right side partially paralyzed. In Room 23 a pneumonia case requiring oxygen had a special R.N. In Room 25 a Mrs. Sutherland— Dr. Smith's patient—was in for a second operation and was suffering pre-surgery jitters. The room across the hall was completely vacant, though a new patient of Dr. Bowen's was to be admitted around noon.

In the little conference room, Kathy went over the charts with the rest of the team. She gave Mary Cranshaw Mrs. Sutherland's chart to study.

"She had a restless night," Kathy said. "Stay with her until time for her surgery. Her operation is scheduled for noon. The three of us can handle the other patients."

"Sure thing," Tillie said.

Mrs. Stein made no comment. She sat stiffly, with hands folded. "Like a child on the first day of school," Kathy thought uncomfortably.

But baths and breakfasts for the patients soon put the aide out of her mind. The morning rush was over and Kathy was going down the corridor for her coffee break when she heard her name called.

"Martin! Martin, come here!" It was Mary Cranshaw's voice from the half-closed door of Room 25.

Mary was standing at the foot of her patient's bed. She beckoned with her hand, but did not turn her eyes.

"Breathe, Mrs. Sutherland," Mary ordered.

The bedclothes rose and fell slightly, almost imperceptibly, as the woman sighed once. Then her breathing stopped.

"Thank goodness you passed by, Martin!" Mary spoke hurriedly. "I couldn't leave. Breathe, Mrs. Sutherland. Take a deep breath—"

Again the deep sigh. Again the dead silence. The patient seemed to be in a coma, yet she appeared to respond to Mary's voice.

"How long has she been like this?"

"I gave her the first pre-op medicine indicated. Ten minutes later, she—she stopped breathing." Mary's own breath was coming in gasps.

"You're sure there was no mistake in medication, Cranshaw?"

Mary shook her head. "Breathe, Mrs. Sutherland. She only takes a breath when I tell her to, Kathy. I don't think I gave her anything wrong—"

"Keep going!" Kathy turned and ran to the Nurses' Station and called the switchboard. "Get us a doctor, stat, Second West. Thanks."

"Doctor Stat, calling Doctor Stat." The operator's voice came at once over the loudspeaker, in the familiar, calm singsong used for calling Dr. Jones or Dr. Smith or Dr. Brown. Only medical personnel knew that "stat" was the abbreviation for "immediately," and was the emergency signal for the nearest physician to come from anywhere in the hospital. "Doctor Stat," the voice said again.

Kathy looked around. Mrs. Rice was nowhere to be seen. Had Cranshaw given the wrong medication? The wrong amount? Reliable, dependable Mary? Still—a Junior nurse—and there was always the margin of human error. Kathy ran back to the room. *Team leader,* she thought bitterly, *and I don't know a thing to do!*

To the two frightened girls in crisp, blue-striped student uniforms standing together at the foot of the bed, it seemed an age before a doctor appeared.

"Breathe, Mrs. Sutherland—" The deep sigh and then the awful silence.

"A case of hysteria," the young resident physician said, after a hurried examination. "Keep the patient breathing, Nurse." He turned to Kathy and ordered a stimulant.

When she returned with the small glass of colorless liquid, the patient had begun to weep.

"She had kept her fears of surgery to herself a little too long. Her way out was to stop breathing," the doctor explained. "Fear can do funny things."

"Then it wasn't due to the medicine?" Mary wiped her eyes. "I was almost sure I hadn't made a mistake. I looked at the chart, and checked the medicine card with the name on the bed, and—and everything. And I couldn't leave to get help, and then Martin came by and she's my team leader—"

The doctor looked at the serious young faces with sympathy. It was not so very long ago that he had been an intern weighted down with the responsibility of new experiences.

"You girls did just the right things," he said, taking the glass from Kathy's hand and skillfully getting the patient to swallow the liquid. "Stay with her and try to reassure her," he said. "I'll get in touch with her own doctor."

The physician had just gone when Mrs. Stein appeared in the door.

"A new patient for Room 21, Miss Martin," she said without a glance at the woman in the bed.

"Dr. Bowen's patient," Kathy murmured half-aloud. "But I can't leave Cranshaw here alone." She looked worriedly at the aide in the doorway. "Do you know the routine for admitting, Mrs. Stein? Get name, address, and so forth. List valuables. Put the patient in bed and make as comfortable as possible."

"I am acquainted with the duties of an admitting nurse, Miss Martin."

"Okay, admit the patient, please."

Kathy watched Mrs. Stein turn stiffly away, and sighed. Perhaps it would have been better to entrust Dr. Bowen's patient to Mary.

"I can manage alone, Cranshaw," she whispered. "First impressions are so important. I'd rather you admit 'd Bowen's patient. Just tell Mrs. Stein you'll take over."

Mrs. Sutherland was almost asleep and breathing normally, but she was holding tight to Kathy's hand as if even in her sleep she needed reassurance.

"On your way to 21, see what Tillie is up to," Kathy said. "I haven't heard her prancing up and down."

Mary stopped hesitantly in the doorway. "You mustn't take team leadership too hard, Martin."

Kathy grinned, suddenly on top of her job again. "Remember what the book says: 'The team leader should at all times identify with members of her group.' I feel as if I'm leading three lives—and none of them my own!"

CHAPTER IV

The Third-Floor Gang

After the first few days, the Seniors settled down for a month of comparative calm. There was a flurry of excitement when the new class of Probationers came to tea at the Senior Residence. But "Probies" were the responsibility of their Big Sisters, the Juniors; of Miss Wilson, the School Director; and of Miss Seaforth, the instructor in Nursing Arts. The fifteen Seniors in the old Merriweather mansion were left pretty much to their own devices. Their classes at State College were not scheduled to begin until the end of September. Except for their eight hours at the hospital, their time was their own.

Housekeeping soon ceased to be a romantic adventure, and turned into something of a chore. Most of the students abandoned the struggle with the out-of-date gas stove and battered pots and pans, and went back to eating all their meals at the hospital cafeteria.

The "third-floor gang," as Kathy and Kelley, Gail and Linda, and Jenny and Yo called themselves, still subscribed to Miss Merriweather's cross-stitched motto on the kitchen wall: "There's no place like home." They scrubbed and vacuumed and ate home-cooked Sunday dinners around the golden-oak kitchen table.

But on weekdays not even roommates saw much of each other. Gail and Yo were on PM shift, and Jenny was still putting in her free hours at the cannery, so that she could make enough money to carry her through the winter.

On the day shift the rule was early to bed, because the girls had to be up at dawn. On PM duty you got home a little after eleven and were glad to kick your shoes off, have a quick glass of milk and tumble into bed.

It was quite outside of the established routine for Kathy to be letting herself into the dark hall on a Thursday at midnight. But Steve Kovak had appeared unexpectedly at supper time.

"I haven't seen you for a month, and when those college courses begin you'll bury yourself in books," he had said. And he had carried Kathy off for dinner and a movie.

It was good to sit across the table from Steve and listen to his humorous, easy-going comments on her tales about Tillie and Mrs. Stein and her trials as a team leader on Second West, and later to laugh together in the balcony of the theater. The evening had been thoroughly satisfying, and Kathy was still smiling as she let herself into the house. She started up the stairs quietly, expecting everyone to be asleep.

Suddenly sepulchral tones floated up the stair well.

"Double, double toil and trouble.
Fire burn and cauldron bubble."

Kathy stopped short. It was Kelley's voice, and it seemed to come from the kitchen.

"Adder's fork and blind-worm's sting—"

"What sort of witches' brew are you stirring up, Lady Macbeth Jones?" Kathy called, as she turned toward the kitchen door.

"Glue, not brew," Yo answered. She was dangling her legs from the top of the old-fashioned sideboard, drinking a cup of hot cocoa. She was still in uniform, and no one could have guessed from her trim appearance that she had just come from eight hours' grueling duty in First Aid.

Kelley, at the stove, just shook her head and continued her weird incantations.

"Lizard's leg and—and— Come on over here and pour me another tablespoon of boiling water, Martin," she said without looking up. "I bought this new kind of fancy mix-it-yourself glue for the bean mosaics. 'Mix-it-yourself! No trouble at all!' I've turned the kitchen into a glue factory!"

"Smells like a glue factory, too," Jenny complained. "I can't tell whether I'm drinking coffee or melted horse's hoofs."

Jenny and Linda, across the table, were in robes and pajamas. Linda's curls were masked in a net, from which bobby pins protruded like miniature daggers as she bent over a bunch of tan, green and red-striped cards, lost in deep concentration.

"Double, double toil and trouble." Kelley began her incantation once more.

This time it was Linda who interrupted. She was close to tears. "You call *that* toil and trouble? Do you realize I have to get all these code numbers and class numbers and instructors' names and everything filled out to turn in tomorrow? Registration gets me so muddled I can't even remember my own name!"

Yo slid down off the sideboard, balancing her cup so deftly that not a drop of cocoa spilled.

"Poor Garfield," she said. "It's a psychological block. Let me help you."

Gratefully, Linda handed over the papers. "Last year Jim said that if I had to pass a course in how to register at State, I'd never get out of school. He ought to have waited until I was an R.N. before he transferred to Berkeley for his pre-med course."

Yo nodded, a twinkle in her eyes. "Get the ink eradicator, child. You've signed your own name where the instructor's belongs!"

Linda got up obediently, but stopped at the stove with sudden interest in Kelley's project.

"I never saw a bean mosaic," she said. "Is it for your room?"

"Heavens, no!" With one hand Kelley pulled a handful

of sketches out of her smock pocket. "Cats, dogs, birds—all for the Pedie ward."

"Oh, Jonesy, the children will love them!" Linda forgot her own troubles in her delight at Kelley's drawings.

"Have to do something to get those kids out of my hair," Kelley grumbled, stirring furiously. But the other girls were on to her. They knew the thought and love that went into her work in the Pediatric ward.

"Ink eradicator!" Yo spoke with a sharpness unusual for her, and Linda padded away on her errand.

"'Legal Aspects of Nursing.'" Jenny studied one of the IBM registration cards. "I'm really scared of that course."

"So am I," Kathy said, unexpectedly. "All that business about what you do as a witness in court, and how to take care of valuables and narcotics—when the doctor is liable and what the nurse's responsibility is on reporting errors—"

Kelley turned off the gas and held up the pot of sticky mucilage in triumph. "I know one thing about responsibility," she said, "but I didn't learn it at the college. The R.N.'s expect the Senior nurse to take the rap for every mistake that happens. When an R.N. slips up, we're 'those irresponsible students.' When a Junior or an aide does something wrong, it's our fault because we're 'responsible team leaders.'"

"It'll get worse when the Probies begin hospital duty," Kathy agreed. She was always ready to talk about the problems of team leadership, but just then Linda reappeared with the bottle of ink eradicator. Trailing close behind was Gail. She was bright-eyed and wide awake, though she'd gone to bed hours before.

"I was just wondering," Gail began. "I mean—Matt's coming tomorrow for the opening of college, and he's asked me to go to meet his aunt in San Francisco on Sunday, and . . ."

"Henderson has come down to earth long enough to worry about what she ought to wear," Linda explained as she sat down at the table again.

"Your blue dress and my white topper," Kelley said with authority.

"My agate bracelet," Kathy put in. "And do your hair in bangs."

Kathy glanced down a little ruefully at the sweater and skirt she had worn on her date with Steve. She hadn't bothered to change, nor had she given a thought to her looks all evening. But then, she had known Steve a long time—and Gail had met Christopher Matthews just last year, when he was adviser for the college paper and she was reporting the Nursing School news. On their first double date, he and Steve had hit it off well, and they had had many foursomes through the winter and spring. Then Gail had gone home to Nevada for the summer vacation. She had come back with a bundle of letters from Matt, postmarked New York, and her head in the clouds. Gail was in love, all right.

But what *was* love anyhow? Kathy did not know. Identifying yourself with the one you loved? But what did "identify" really mean? The book on nursing arts said that a team leader should at all times *identify* with members of her group—and that just meant you were responsible for what anyone on your team did. She was still puzzling over the question when she trailed Kelley and the precious pot of glue up the two flights of stairs.

"You're quiet as a clam," Kelley said as they unpeeled the studio couches that served for beds. "Didn't you and Steve have a good time?"

"Yes, we did. But Gail set me to thinking deep thoughts. All about love and identity." Kathy laughed. "I was wondering how I could be expected to 'identify' with a scared rabbit."

"Mrs. Stein?"

"Yes. By the way, Gail was right. That mop of red hair *is* a wig."

right for the patient to have just a little glass of water?
(Kathy had seized the glass of water just in time, and
later had explained to the frightened Probie that NPO
means nothing—nothing at all—by mouth, and how dangerous it could be if there was anything in the patient's
stomach during an operation.)

By the end of the first day, none of the Seniors liked
to remember that they, too, had once been Probies. The
second day had been different. The Probies had lost
their stage fright and pulled themselves together. And
Kathy rapidly found herself bragging about her Probie,
Helen Gleason.

At Wednesday morning's conference, she assigned
tasks to Gleason without misgivings. The beds were all
occupied and there was plenty for everybody to do—
more than enough when Dr. Johnson appeared to make
his rounds. It was the team leader's job to accompany
the doctor. But that meant a quick reassignment of duties.

"Please take over from Cranshaw in Room 21," she
said to Mrs. Stein, who had brought the word of Dr.
Johnson's unexpected arrival. "She must be almost finished with Mrs. Thomas' bath and I need her in here."

It was not until after mid-morning nourishments that
Kathy had a minute to sit down at the desk and look over
her charts. She had Mrs. Marcelene Thomas' chart in
her hand when Dr. Bowen strolled up and laid a rainbow-
colored sheaf of laboratory slips before her.

"Results of Mrs. Thomas' latest tests," he said.

Kathy groaned. "Where are we going to put them, Doctor? Look at this chart!"

"Squeeze 'em in," Bowen answered cheerfully. "They're the last. She's going home today—after lunch. Her sister will come for her at two p.m. Just in time, too. I need the bed. Don't look so gleeful. It's not for myself. I'm the picture of health, thank you."

Bowen was one of the younger physicians, good-looking in a Cary Grant sort of way. He was just the type that student nurses were said to fall in love with. He had a large practice, yet never seemed in a hurry, and was always ready with a long anecdote when anyone would listen. Nevertheless, most of the nurses ducked when they saw him coming. They found his frequent jokes and wisecracks hard to take. Kathy had forgiven him for his sense of humor, however, since he had bought Kelley's painting last year.

"How's that roommate of yours, by the way?" Bowen said. "Still neglecting her painting to play with groceries?"

Kathy smiled. "You really should pay a visit to the Pedie Ward if you want to see what Jonesy has been doing with her rice and beans, Dr. Bowen."

"Not I. I'm afraid I'd be converted to mosaics—and I hate 'em!"

Kathy watched him swing down the hall to the elevator. Then, charts in hand, she unlocked the narcotics cupboard to set out the pre-operative medications. She was

Mrs. Rice put down the phone. "Dr. Johnson anticipates no unfavorable reactions. He was very understanding," she said, but there was no sympathy in her voice. An error in medication was a serious thing even if no harm was done. "Make out your report in triplicate, Miss Martin."

Kathy nodded. One report would go to the doctor, one to the hospital supervisor, the third to Miss Wilson, head of the Nursing School. Kathy had followed all the rules of safety and then let her hand play tricks on her. That came from hurrying.

She walked slowly to the narcotics cupboard, returned the unused demerol, recorded the return, and prepared another medication for Mrs. Black. She made out the report of error and laid it before the head nurse. Then, just ahead of the tray girl bringing the lunches, she went back to administer Mrs. Black's medication.

She noted that Tillie and Mrs. Stein were supervising lunches, that Cranshaw was assisting with an IV—an intravenous feeding—in 23, and crossed the hall to Mrs. Marcelene Thomas' door to tell her the good news that she was going home.

Mrs. Thomas was sitting up in bed with her tray across her knees, eating with zest. But as soon as she caught sight of a nurse with a cap on, she began complaining.

"They forgot *again*," she said, "that I like lemon with my lamb chop. I should think you could get better kitchen help, Miss Martin, considering—"

Mrs. Thomas had been in the hospital for over a month. She was a fussy, demanding patient, and Kathy would not be sorry to see her go.

"I'll get you a slice of lemon, Mrs. Thomas."

"Oh, never mind. My chop would be cold by the time you brought it. I just thought you'd like to know how careless they are."

"I'll come back when you finish lunch to help you get dressed, Mrs. Thomas. Dr. Bowen says you can go home today. Your sister is coming for you at two o'clock."

There was a flash of pleasure, then discontent clouded the woman's eyes. "Sue will probably be late—she always is. And don't forget to give me back the rings and watch that nurse took away the day I came in."

"They're quite safe in the vault." Kathy tried to speak patiently. "Eat your lunch now and have a rest. Then we'll get you all fixed up."

Kathy ate her own lunch in gloomy solitude, stopped at the office to pick up her patient's dismissal card and canvas bag of valuables, and hurried back to Second West.

By a quarter of two, Dr. Bowen's patient was dressed and ready. Her bag was packed, and in silk dress and high-heeled shoes she sat by the window. She looked, for the moment, almost contented. Kathy realized that Mrs. Thomas must once have been very pretty. Anxious to please, she brought the patient a hand mirror.

"See how well you are looking! Now we'll check out your valuables. After you sign the receipt, you'll be all set when your sister comes."

The mirror fell with a splintering crash. "My locket!" Mrs. Thomas clutched a thin gold chain around her neck. "She stole it! That nurse stole it! She tried to take it away from me the first day I came!"

Kathy stared at the chain. There was no doubt about it: the locket was missing. It had been a nuisance all the time Mrs. Thomas had been in the hospital. The chain had to be removed every time the patient was bathed, every time she had X rays. She had refused to be parted from it. And now the locket was gone from its chain.

"I'm sure we'll find it, Mrs. Thomas." Kathy could not keep the tremor from her voice. She would never like Wednesdays again! She tore the bed to pieces. Then she crawled on the floor, feeling for the small object.

All the while, between moans, Mrs. Thomas talked about its value. The blue stones were star sapphires. She had worn the locket ever since she was a girl, and now that nurse had stolen it.

Nervously, Kathy called Mary in and asked her whether she had seen the locket.

"You tried to take it! The first day." Mrs. Thomas wheeled around as Mary entered the room. Her face was contorted with rage.

"Of course," Mary began. "An admitting nurse—"
She got no further.

"You've had your eyes on it ever since. You took it off when you gave me my bath this morning. And then you put the chain back so I wouldn't notice."

A knock on the door announced Mrs. Thomas' sister, large-bosomed, flurried, a little late after her struggle with highway traffic.

"They've stolen my locket!" Mrs. Thomas brought her sister up to date on all details.

"I thought the hospital kept valuables in a safe." The sister looked at Kathy accusingly.

Mrs. Thomas interrupted. "You know I never take off my locket. I've worn it ever since Papa brought it to me from the Chicago World's Fair."

Kathy slipped away to report the disaster to Mrs. Rice —the second catastrophe in one day! She felt as if she were living through a nightmare. It was unthinkable that Mary could have stolen it. But Mrs. Thomas had not been out of the room, and the locket was not in the room. Mrs. Thomas had had her lunch in bed. And the locket was missing. Not only that, the lost locket was not merely a trinket of sentimental value, as everyone supposed. It was a valuable jewel. And Mary must have been the last person to handle it before it disappeared.

Mrs. Rice listened quietly and sent for the supervisor of the hospital. Together they returned to Mrs. Thomas' room.

Mary stood by the door.

"Was the locket on its chain, Miss Cranshaw, when

you removed it for the bath?" Mrs. Rice asked quietly.

"I—I think so." Mary's eyes sought Kathy's. "It's hard to remember every little thing."

"*Little thing?*" Mrs. Thomas was in tears again. "The chain felt light after my bath. I remember now."

Mary opened her lips as if to speak, then seemed to think better of it. Instead, she turned and ran from the room.

They let her go. The Supervisor took charge.

"Were there other valuables, Miss Martin?"

Kathy held out the bag and the list that Mrs. Thomas had signed—one diamond ring, one wedding ring set in sapphires, one opal ring, a wrist watch. Everything was there, everything safely accounted for—except the locket.

The Supervisor turned again to Kathy. "Why was that valuable locket not put in the vault? Who admitted the patient?"

Mrs. Rice spoke up. "Miss Cranshaw was the admitting nurse, but it was I who permitted Mrs. Thomas to retain the locket. I assumed it to have only sentimental value and as a symbol of security—"

Kathy drew a long breath. It was not unusual to accede to the whims of a nervous patient, but she was relieved that Mrs. Rice remembered the incident. At least Mary had not taken it upon herself to make the decision.

The Supervisor pulled out a pen. "If you will just make a note of the missing jewel, Mrs. Thomas." She spoke soothingly. "We shall make a thorough search for the lost article and keep you informed. A wheel chair, Miss Martin. You may take the patient to the door."

Mrs. Thomas was still sputtering when Kathy helped her into the car. She talked of arresting the thief; she threatened to sue; she said triumphantly that the insurance agent would have a thing or two to say.

Kathy was too disconsolate to answer. It was three o'clock—time for the PM shift to take over. Time for Dr. Bowen's new patient to arrive. She hurried upstairs to write up her charts.

Mrs. Rice looked up from the desk with a sympathetic smile. Things like this happened, she said. There was always the factor of human error.

"You don't think Mary Cranshaw is *guilty?*" Kathy brought out the words with difficulty. Mary was not only her teammate, but her friend.

"I don't know." The older woman drummed thoughtfully on her desk. "I believe in the old Anglo-Saxon doctrine that a person is innocent until proven guilty. I have reported the matter to Miss Wilson. She recommends that we continue to assign duties to Miss Cranshaw as usual."

CHAPTER VI

A Disturbing Disappearance

The team conference next morning was like a double-exposure picture. Kathy talked at top speed about the reports left by the night nurses. Everyone took notes on her jot sheet, and all the while the thoughts of the five were on a single object—a lost locket set with sapphires.

Mary Cranshaw was red-eyed. Mrs. Stein was even more silent and aloof than usual. The Probie tied and untied her stiff necktie nervously. It was Tillie who blurted out what everyone was thinking.

"Look, Miss Martin. About that locket. Has anybody looked through the dirty laundry? My grandpa lost his false teeth last week. He swore somebody in the house had taken them. Bless Pat, I shook out a pillow slip and there were the teeth! Not a whole set you know, just what they call a partial . . ."

"I went through the whole day's laundry, Martin," Mary Cranshaw interrupted nervously. "I stayed after the PM shift came on. I searched the room again, too, while it was being made up for the incoming patient. Gleason helped. I—I thought it would be better for our team if we could find the locket instead of someone else."

Tillie pulled a stick of gum out of her pocket, caught Kathy's eye on her and thrust it regretfully away again. "That locket wasn't so much," she said. "I had it in my hand dozens of times when I was bathing that old pill. I've seen prettier in the five-and-ten."

"We speak of the patients by name, Tillie." Kathy could have hugged the girl for breaking the tension of the conference, but she couldn't let her call Mrs. Thomas an old pill—not in front of a Probie.

"Well, anyway, I bet the—the patient just claimed it was very valuable to make trouble."

"I wish that were true," Kathy said, gathering up the charts. "Mrs. Rice said the locket was insured for quite a large sum. She said an adjuster from the insurance company might want to ask all of us some questions, and if he does we're to answer simply and helpfully—the best we can."

She stood up. The conference was over and Mrs. Stein had not spoken a word. The others filed out, and Mrs. Stein had reached the door when Kathy called her back.

"Can you remember whether the locket was on its chain when you relieved Cranshaw? You finished giving Mrs. Thomas her bath, didn't you—after Dr. Johnson came?"

Kathy fell silent before Mrs. Stein's hostile gaze. "I know nothing," the woman said, and scurried away.

After lunch hour, the insurance adjusters came. Mrs.

Rice called the nurses to be questioned, one at a time. Kathy was the last.

"When did you last see the locket? Did you ever discuss its value? With whom? Under what circumstances? When did you notice it was missing? I understand that you dressed Mrs. Thomas? You were, then, the last person to have access—"

"You're not suggesting that *I* took the thing!" Kathy asked.

"We're not suggesting anything Miss—er—Miss Martin. We're here to get the facts."

"This is how Mary must have felt when *she* was accused of stealing. And how Mrs. Stein must have felt when I questioned her this morning," Kathy said to herself miserably. "I'm going to explain to Mrs. Stein that I didn't mean to sound like an accuser."

Lights were popping over the doors up and down the corridor. Mr. Guttenberg wanted to be turned over. Mrs. Smith couldn't find her eyeglasses. The pre-op in 25 wanted water, which she couldn't have.

A half hour went by before Kathy had time to look for Mrs. Stein, and then she couldn't be found. No one had seen her. Her raincoat and purse were missing from their hook in the closet. Her jot sheets lay in a neat pile on the conference table. It was still a half-hour before three o'clock—but Mrs. Stein had left the hospital.

Heavy-hearted, Kathy took on the missing aide's duties as well as her own, and finished out the day.

When Kelley came home, Kathy was stretched out on the studio couch, her face buried in the pillow. She was not crying, she was just too discouraged to face a sunlit world.

"Don't you see that this clears Mary completely?" Kelley said when she had heard Kathy's story. "The Stein woman is obviously the thief."

Kathy shook her head. "I never liked Mrs. Stein, but her leaving the hospital in the middle of her duties doesn't prove that she's guilty—and anyway, she's a member of my team, guilty or innocent. Besides, Cranshaw is the one Mrs. Thomas accused. She's the one who's going to be under a cloud until the locket is found. And there were lots of other people around, too."

"The police will go to Stein's house with a search warrant and that will be the end of it," Kelley said firmly.

"It's not just Mrs. Stein," Kathy said. "Look at my record as a team leader! I wouldn't blame Miss Wilson if she refused to let me graduate."

"Nonsense. But you won't be worth living with unless we clear this up quickly. Get on your feet and go over to the office and wangle Stein's home address from somebody. I'll get hold of Gail and Linda. This is a job for the Do-It-Yourself Detective Agency."

"What good will it do to see that wretched woman?" Kathy objected. "Even if she *does* have the locket, she's not going to just hand it over to us." But she quickly ran a comb through her hair and fumbled for her lipstick.

Anything at all was better than lying there and brooding.

When Kathy came back with Mrs. Stein's address in her purse, she found a sign on her door in Linda's handwriting:

TEMPORARY OFFICE
Double Scoop Ice Cream Parlor
Operator Martin, please report immediately.

DIYDA

As usual, Linda was fortifying herself with an ice-cream soda. No wonder she never lost weight! Kathy slipped out of her uniform and into a sweater and skirt, and dashed around the corner.

Linda, Gail and Kelley were perched on stools at the counter of the little shop.

"We ordered you a milkshake," Linda said. "Did you get the address?"

"Yes. It's across town. Two buses. Are you sure you want to go?"

"Nor snow, nor hail, nor rain, nor the San Tomás transportation system shall keep us from our duty!" Gail declaimed, with suitable gestures.

Kathy smiled for the first time that day. "What are we going to say? Or do? When we get there, I mean."

"Never mind that. We'll think of something."

It was almost dark before they finally found the street and number on Kathy's paper, and when they did it proved to be not a house at all, but a sprawling brown garage with rooms above. Kelley rang a bell beside the scarred green door that seemed to belong to the upstairs apartment. After a moment they could hear footsteps on creaking stairs. A large, gray-haired woman opened the door.

"Mrs. Stein?" she repeated after Kathy. "She don't live here any more. Her and her daughter left today—soon as the girl came home from school. I rent by the week, see, and like I told her, the week ain't up till Saturday. So I couldn't give no refund. You know how it is."

The landlady seemed quite willing to spin out her tale indefinitely. But Kelley interrupted to ask Mrs. Stein's new address.

"What do you know about that! She forgot to leave one. It's most likely somewhere near where she works. You know the San Tomás Hospital? You get her address from the hospital. That's where her job is. And if you know anybody wants a nice room with kitchen privileges—"

Kathy started to explain that Mrs. Stein no longer worked at the hospital. But what was the use? She had stolen the locket and given them all the slip.

The door closed.

"End of Do-It-Yourself Detective Agency," Gail said crisply. "If you ask me, Martin, I'd say that we'll never see that locket—or your aide—again."

CHAPTER VII

Gail Steals the Show

Rain, after the long months of cloudless skies, came early in November. Kathy had been on the PM shift in First Aid for a week. Splashing home in the darkness, she welcomed the change of weather. On the ranch, rain before Christmas was a cause for rejoicing. For her father it meant an end to irrigation. And for Steve, an end to troublesome and dangerous autumn forest fires. Maybe now he could get away from the Fire Department for the weekend of the Senior Show!

Except for the dripping eaves, the old Merriweather house was quiet. The girls on morning shift were in bed. "Or out on Friday-night dates," Kathy said to herself.

Kelley and Yo wouldn't be home for an hour. They had been assigned to six weeks' duty at the state mental hospital, which was an hour's bus trip from town.

Kathy made herself a cup of instant coffee, but she didn't linger in the lonesome kitchen. Mug in hand, she climbed up to her third-floor room, brushed a scattering of Kelley's eternal rice grains off the desk and sat down to satisfy her yearning for home with one of her rare letters to the family. "Talking papers," her mother called them, remembering the Indian lore she had studied at school.

Page after page was covered with Kathy's hurried scrawl.

. . . It seems odd to be back in First Aid—a kind of double-take from the months I spent in the Emergency Ward as a lowly aide in the Appleton Hospital that time Papa was hurt. Somehow I keep expecting to see Tony Ellsworth brought in on a stretcher. That's an experience I wouldn't want to live through again! But what good things have happened to Tony since then! Do you suppose he'll come back to ranching after the Army? Maybe not, since you write that he's being given special training in mechanics.

It's funny to have all of us growing up. School is so close to the end that we're all beginning to say "Where to?" and "What next?" Like Nick deciding whether to take that scholarship at Agricultural College next year. (I hope you do, Nick!

Mid-terms are coming up and we've got to decide before long what Senior Service to apply for. (That's the special training we take for the different fields of nursing. It's the one time we have a free choice of duties.)

Jenny's having no problem. She's been headed from the first for Public Health. Kelley will go for nursing children, I imagine—unless she ups and marries Dr. Bowen! I can see they're interested in each other even though the hospital frowns on doctors paying any attention to us student nurses. Linda, who wears Jim's fraternity pin over her heart when she thinks we're not looking, is in Surgical now and loving it. She'll probably choose that for her Senior Service.

As usual, your daughter is torn twenty ways. Why wasn't I born with blinders on my eyes and a mind that stayed made up? Steve always says I take things too hard, and maybe I do. We still haven't heard anything more from that aide I wrote you about—Mrs. Stein. I was glad to get away from Second West and forget her. But I'd feel better if that awful locket would show up.

We're having a dreadful time getting the Senior Show ready for December. Gail, our theatrical expert, spends all her writing time making fancy doodles that spell "Matt." And Kelley uses her spare minutes gluing grains of rice on a canvas—some kind of experiment in rice and India ink. This occasionally makes for strained relations because of rice on chairs and desks and in my bed, and the smell of glue is—well—pretty gluey. But I have to admit the kneeling figure on the canvas across the room is strong, dramatic and (blessed thought!) almost done. What is going to happen to the show, nobody knows.

Kathy was chewing the end of her pencil, with a fresh sheet of paper before her, when Kelley and Yo came in. The letter was abandoned. This matter of the Senior Show was serious.

"I haven't an idea in my head," she said mournfully.

"Who wants ideas in the middle of the night?" Kelley threw her wet raincoat on the chair. "We had to wait an hour for the bus. I'm drenched."

Kathy watched the puddle of water drip from Kelley's raincoat onto scattered grains of rice. "Are you cooking chow mein?" she asked a little bitterly.

"It's a lovely rain for the strawberries," Yo said.

"You country gals!" Rain to Kelley was nothing but wet clothes and having to reset her hair. "What don't you have an idea in your head about, Martin? Anyway, do you know it's almost one o'clock?"

Kathy ignored the last remark. They could sleep as late as they liked tomorrow.

"I was writing a letter home," she began, "and I got to thinking about the Senior Show. It's only four weeks away!"

"We can all go as mermaids if this rain keeps up," Kelley answered. "Or pajama girls," she said as the door creaked open, revealing a sleep-flushed Linda in pink pajamas.

"Do you realize how late it is?" Linda said. "Gail's not home from the movies!"

"Dear, dear," Kelley scoffed. "What *will* Miss Merriweather say?"

"The same thing she always says—nothing. Merriweather is the ideal housemother." Kathy was only mildly interested.

But Kelley had a gleam in her eye. She snatched up Kathy's blank sheet of paper and began writing.

"Special reprimand for Miss Henderson," she said. "How's this? We'll put it on the bulletin board."

TO: Miss Henderson:

FROM: Committee of Instructors
        San Tomás School of Nursing

We would like to speak to you on matters of health and ethical standards: viz., late hours in the company of a certain gentleman.

You will please attend a hearing between the hours of 1 a.m. and 3 a.m. on this day, November 21.

The three girls were tacking the notice at a conspicuous spot on the bulletin board when Matt's car drove up to the door.

"Quick—behind the parlor door!" Kelley ordered.

They needn't have fled in such haste. There was a long wait before Gail tiptoed into the hall alone. They saw her stop, lean closer to read the notice, gasp, and then chuckle.

"All right, Henderson," Kelley said. "Come and prepare for cross-examination."

But Gail stole Kelley's show after all. Wordlessly, she held out the fourth finger of her left hand.

"Gail! A real-for-sure solitaire diamond!" Even Kelley was impressed. It was the first engagement in their crowd.

Linda was so carried away that she dashed to the piano and, forgetful of the hour, began pounding out the wedding march from *Lohengrin*.

Naturally, the whole house was awakened. Students on the morning shift, fresh after hours in bed, others blurry-eyed from their first deep sleep trooped into the parlor. Ann Cooper, the class president, tried halfheartedly to restore order.

No one heard the door of Miss Merriweather's wing open. No one saw the housemother patter across the hall until she appeared at the parlor door, in boudoir cap and a velvet robe.

"Is the house on fire? Have you given the alarm?"

Before anyone could explain, Gail astonished herself, Miss Merriweather, and the entire Senior class by throwing her arms around the old lady and holding out her left hand so that the diamond would catch the light.

"His name is Christopher Matthews, but everybody calls him Matt. He's doing graduate work in journalism. We'll be married after graduation."

Miss Merriweather nodded and smiled, suddenly went shy again and sidled out of the room.

"If you'd been alone with her, Gail, I'm sure you'd have gotten the story of her life," Ann Cooper said.

> *I was about to marry a sailor.*
> *I was in love like you.*
> *And on my wedding night*
> *My lover was lost on the ocean blue.*

Linda recited with a few suitable chords on the piano.

Kelley shook her head. "He was a roofer and fell off the roof while she waited at the church."

"Poor old thing. Do you really suppose—" Kathy cut off her words. Across the heads of the others she saw Miss Merriweather's door opening again.

The old lady came slowly now, and diffidently. She walked up to Gail and put a yellowed lace handkerchief in her hand. "For you, my dear. It was my mother's bridal kerchief—and now, off to bed, young ladies."

Next day on the bulletin board a new announcement appeared:

ENGAGEMENT PARTY

TIME: Saturday night
PLACE: The Mask and Dagger
GUESTS OF HONOR: C. Matthews and G. Henderson.
P.S. *Bring your man, if you've got one.*

The "Mask and Dagger" was not as elaborate as its name. It was, in fact, a little hole-in-the-wall coffee shop, but very popular with the State College students. There was good entertainment of the home-grown, do-it-yourself variety. The customers brought guitars or banjos or bongo drums, and sang folk songs or blues. You could buy hot spiced cider or espresso coffee or Italian chocolate. If you wanted food, you had to bring it along.

On the evening of the party a life-size portrait of Matt and Gail decorated one wall. Matt, in approved *Front Page* newspaper-office style, had his feet on a desk and a typewriter balanced dangerously on his knees. A hat was tilted on the back of his head, and a thermometer —tastefully decorated with cupids—hung out of the corner of his mouth. The mercury stood at 110. A solici-

tous Gail, in uniform and cap made entirely of newspapers, stood by, taking his pulse.

Jim Telford came down from Berkeley; Steve drove up
from Appleton. The Senior Nurses and an assortment of
Matt's journalism friends from State crowded the Mask
and Dagger to the doors. An enormous cheesecake was
brought in, topped with a bride and groom. As Gail and
Matt rose to cut the cake with a paper knife, Kelley added the finishing touch—a shower of varicolored rice.

"My last box," Kelley said, with the air of a martyr.

"Thank goodness for that," Kathy whispered to Steve.
The evening was almost over—the last crumb of cake
eaten, the last song sung.

Suddenly Gail looked brightly around. "Has anybody
done anything about the Senior Variety Show?" she
asked. A groan went up from the tables.

"Have you looked in our wastebaskets?" Faith Loring
said. "Reams of ideas—hundreds of rhymes—all bad."

"*Scene:* The Mask and Dagger," Gail mumbled, and
reached for a pencil, then remembered that she was in an
evening dress. No pocket, no pencil. "Give me a pencil
and a sheet of paper, Matt darling."

Matter-of-factly, Matt supplied both.

"Do you like soft music while you work?" Steve asked.
"I'll oblige on the bongo drums."

"*Shh,*" Kathy whispered. "Let genius burn. We really
need that script."

CHAPTER VIII

Disaster

"Ramirez," said Kathy, "you look more like a patient than a nurse. What have they been doing to you up in Surgery?" She looked across the table with genuine concern. Lines of fatigue pulled down Jenny's mouth, and her long, slender hands trembled visibly as she lifted a bowl of soup from the tray.

Jenny tried to smile. "Five hours as scrub nurse on an exploratory stomach operation. They found what they were looking for—a tumor, malignant. Removed as much as they dared."

"Those long operations can be exhausting, all right," Kathy said sympathetically.

"Not always," Jenny said. "Only this time—well, the surgeon was ready to close up. And then, without any warning, the patient was gone. Just—just snuffed out like a candle." Jenny shook her head. "He wasn't old. I saw his wife when we brought him up to the O.R. 'Now don't you worry,' I said to her. 'There's not a thing to worry about.' Well, I had to say *something!*" Abruptly she pushed away the untouched bowl of soup.

"You eat that soup." Kathy spoke slowly and firmly, as if she were giving orders to Johnny. One of the tasks of student nurses was keeping each other on an even keel. It was one of the things that made them a close-knit sisterhood.

Jenny obediently picked up her spoon. "That's what Miss Johnson said. She sent me down here. She was making Dr. Lasser some tea."

"Oh, were you on with Johnson? She's a terrific surgical nurse."

"She certainly is. She has to be, you know."

"How do you mean, 'has to be'?"

Jenny looked at Kathy thoughtfully. "Your grandmother came from Europe—right?"

"Right."

"And had trouble with the language, and it wasn't easy for her?"

"Right."

"Well, nobody today thinks of your family as anything but just plain Americans. You belong. But if you're a Negro, like Miss Johnson, or even a little darker than the average, like my people, with mixed-up Indian and Spanish ancestors, or Oriental-looking, like Yo—well, the way things are, you have to work harder to make your performance better than other people's. To be accepted. At least that's the way it is now. It won't always be like that."

Kathy realized what she hadn't known—that Jenny

and Yo and Miss Johnson did have special problems. She nodded slowly, hating to admit the unpleasant truth. Thoughtfully, she glanced outside and stood up. "Wow! It's dark already. I have to get back to First Aid. Nothing much to do during the day, but about dusk, accidents are apt to start rolling in."

"Don't forget about arranging your trade-off for Senior Show next week," Jenny said.

"Not likely! Suppose Gail hadn't come off her cloud! Do you realize she's written and directed every show in our three years at school?"

Jenny nodded. "Don't breathe it, but Cooper is going to send Gail American Beauty roses from the class!"

•   •   •

Kathy was scrubbing instruments half an hour later when the blast came. It sounded far-off, but it shook up the equipment trays and knocked a beaker off the shelf.

Sirens followed almost immediately, and then the shrill ring of the telephone.

"Explosion in a cannery on North Main," a singsong voice said. "Get ready for anything."

A moment later the loudspeakers were calling "Doctor Stat to First Aid, Doctor Stat, please," with monotonous regularity. Nurses and aides who could be spared from other floors hurried in. The blood bank was opened, Central Supply double-staffed. The distant wail of a siren grew louder.

Before the first victim was brought in, the supervising

nurse from Second East came to take charge. The phone rang again. The same voice said that they were clearing the decks in surgery.

The first patient brought in was in shock, cut by flying glass. The second was even more seriously hurt. Her steam burns gave an indication of worse to come.

"Send an aide for plasma in Room A," the nurse-in-charge directed Kathy. "Take admittance yourself. Establish identity where possible, notify next of kin."

The victims came in ambulances, in private cars. They came in greater numbers than Kathy could handle. She was grateful to hear Miss Johnson's voice at her side. "I'll help you admit," she said. "You take one, I'll take the next. Give priority to the DI's."

They worked smoothly side by side—the experienced surgical nurse and the student. Almost two hours went by. Still the victims came in a never-ending stream.

Two orderlies set down the next patient and hurried off. A third stayed, his thumb pressed over the wounded man's arm. When he released his hold for a moment, bright red blood squirted over his cuff. A severed artery! And the patient's face was already gray and drawn. No time for questions of identity now.

"Doctor, over here!" Kathy's voice was urgent.

No response.

She glanced again at the patient. Blood—whole blood —was going to be needed. An injection of glucose and water in the veins should be started before much more blood was lost. And a tourniquet on the arm that was cut. Tourniquet first? Or blood-typing for transfusion? "Keep holding that cut," Kathy directed the orderly, and turned to Miss Johnson. The surgical nurse was bending over an inert figure with short fuzzy hair. A woman, Kathy realized, though the short hair was more like a man's. She was dreadfully burned.

Miss Johnson was whispering in the woman's ear, trying to reach through to her. "Helene . . . Helene . . ."

"Miss Johnson—"

The older nurse glanced up at Kathy and then at the orderly bent over the man on the stretcher.

"Lab man!" Miss Johnson's voice was short.

A young man in a white coat hurried over.

"Identify blood type and cross-match for five units for Martin's patient!" Miss Johnson wasn't waiting for doctor's orders. "Martin, get a tourniquet. I'll find a doctor to start IV's on both these patients. And I'll have somebody take over admitting."

Kathy was putting on the tourniquet when a doctor hurried over. Working as a team, the doctor and Miss Johnson started plasma transfusion on the unconscious woman. Then the doctor turned to examine Kathy's patient.

"Get this one typed and cross-matched for whole-blood transfusion. Looks like four or five units," the doctor said. "We'll start glucose and water immediately."

Kathy noticed that Miss Johnson didn't mention that

she had already asked for the blood. No unnecessary words were spoken.

The standard with the bottle of distilled water was at the patient's side when the technician went by, his white coat ballooning out in his haste. "O-negative"— he flung out the words. "Did you say five units? We've only got one unit in the blood bank. I'll have to send a call for emergency blood over the radio."

The stream of patients was down to a trickle. Kathy was admitting again, when a police officer in uniform breezed in. "Heard you needed O blood. That's my type."

Gratefully, Kathy motioned him across the hall to the laboratory.

A few minutes later he came out of the laboratory door. "I'm O type, all right, but not negative. Sorry."

It was a relief to hear the booming voice, to listen to the man's firm, healthy strides as he strode away.

A taxi driver was next. "I was cruising with my radio on. You still need O-negative blood? That's me."

"I'll go back on admittance," Miss Johnson said. "You'd better carry through on your man's transfusion."

Kathy led the donor to the lab. Blood type, O.K. Cross-match, satisfactory. She left the man triumphantly peeling off his coat and went out to see if there were other volunteers. They'd need more of the rare-type blood than one donor could give.

A young woman in a camel's-hair coat was standing

at the door, a boy of eighteen months or so in her arms. "I'm O blood type, Rh negative," the woman explained. "I came as soon as I could—but I didn't have anybody I could leave with Timmy. I had to bring him along."

Kathy smiled, though every muscle of her body was aching with fatigue. "I'll take care of the boy," she said.

"It was so awful hearing about all those poor people. I'm so glad I can be of use." The young woman transferred her twenty-five-pound load to Kathy's arms. Tim grinned and promptly knocked her cap askew. The mother scarcely noticed. She moved toward the lab with what Steve would have called a Florence Nightingale look in her eyes.

Kathy managed to keep the youngster quiet while the mother gave her pint of blood and sipped a cup of tea to restore her body fluids. Then the child began to cry.

"You'll have to rest a little longer," Kathy said to the mother. "Take Tim in your lap. I'll get him some milk if you like."

She rushed off to the cafeteria. In the corridor, a steel cart was in her way. Without slowing down, she veered, slipped, and fell against the corner of a door.

"I'm all right," Kathy said to no one in particular. She got to her feet and continued, a little shakily, toward the cafeteria. Dr. Bowen met her near the cafeteria door. He stopped, looked puzzled, pulled out a handkerchief and wiped off a trickle of blood running down her cheek.

"What happened to you?"

"I just bumped my head. I'm okay."

"Come over here to the light. I want to look at the pupils of your eyes," he said. Then, "Go up to Second West. Tell them to put you to bed. That's an order, Miss Martin."

The doctor led her, protesting, to the elevator and pressed the button.

CHAPTER IX

Kathy Is a Patient

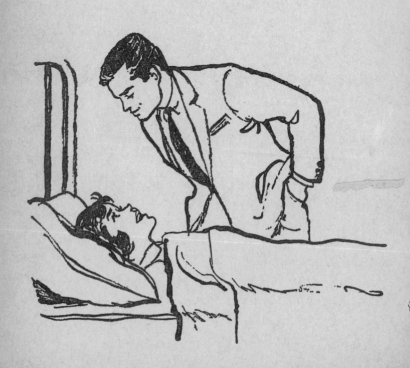

Kathy didn't remember getting out of the elevator. She didn't remember anything until she opened her eyes and saw Dr. Bowen talking to someone at the foot of her bed. She was only mildly surprised to see that the someone was her mother. "And there's Steve by the window," she thought. "Or maybe I'm dreaming."

Aloud, she said, "I must have passed out."

"For twelve hours," Dr. Bowen answered succinctly.

"How do you feel?" Kathy could hear the strain in her mother's voice.

"I'm okay, Mom. Really I am." Suddenly she pushed the bedclothes off and tried to get up. "I'm on duty! There was an explosion. A disaster—"

"Lie still, Martin," Dr. Bowen cautioned. "The cut on your scalp is superficial. But you have a concussion." He left the room, and Ella Martin hurried after him.

"But Doctor—" The bed whirled madly round and round. Steve crossed the room and held Kathy's hand. The walls and floor, the bed steadied again.

Kathy giggled nervously.

"What's funny?"

"I'm a *patient*. Isn't that funny, Steve?"

"No," he growled. "And the next time you feel like hitting a door, please use your fists."

"Don't look so worried, Steve. I'll be all right," she said softly.

A Probie in a blue-striped uniform came in, holding a syringe and looking scared.

"Doctor ordered a shot, Martin. May I—is it all right if I give it to you now?"

Kathy remembered only too well how she had felt learning to give IM's—intramuscular hypos. First you practiced on a rubber ball, then on the well-punctured dummy, Miss Mary Chase. That hadn't been hard at all. Then Mrs. Seaforth, the Nursing Arts instructor, had let the Probies practice giving hypos to her. But when you walked into a hospital room and a real patient lay in the bed—that had been different! She smiled at the Probie. "Have you given one before?" she asked.

"Only to Mrs. Seaforth—unless you count Mary Chase!"

"Well, carry on." She noticed the Probie gesturing nervously toward Steve, her face red as a beet.

"Oh, Steve," Kathy said, "will you go out in the hall? This young lady has work to do! Now," she went on, hoping for her own sake to put the girl at ease, "just a quick jab. Pretend I'm Mary Chase . . . Ouch! Good girl. It didn't hurt at all," she lied bravely. The Probie fled with her syringe.

"Maybe it should happen to all Seniors," Kathy said as Steve came through the door. "Being given IM shots by Probies, I mean. Makes you appreciate what your first patients went through."

"Good idea." Steve grinned as he turned a straight chair around and sat down by the bed.

Kathy turned to smile at him, and the sharp pain made her wince.

"Keep your head still." Steve's deep voice was anxious. He was worried when he saw her in pain. "Your mother wants to get back to Appleton, so we'll be leaving in a minute. The doctor thinks you're doing okay, and says you'll be up in a few days. Don't rush it, though. You've got to take care of my girl for me. That's an order."

"Thank you, Doctor. I'll put it on my jot sheet." She smiled drowsily.

She was asleep before Steve left the room. She slept most of the day, opening her eyes now and then to see a different visitor at her bedside. Mrs. Rice, Miss Vale, Miss Wilson, Pete, the orderly. An apparition in gray that proved on a close-up to be Miss Merriweather. And, of course, the girls. They tiptoed in between classes, before going on duty, on coffee break. Kelley and Yo ran in on their way to the bus that would take them to the mental hospital.

"I'm coming back for the night," Kelley said. "I promised your mother. Steve took her back home."

Gail came at supper and stayed through visiting hours.

Kathy had ice packs on each side of her head. It was hard for her to move or talk, but it was good, when she opened her eyes now and then, to know that Gail was in the room. Just before Gail left, she asked about the Senior Show.

"It won't be the same without you," Gail answered. "Loring's going to do your part in the skit. She'll have time to change after her acrobatic dance."

Then the long night began. Kathy started thinking of all sorts of things she wanted to know: Who was the other patient in the room—the one behind the screen? Her head ached. Had Bowen ordered anything if she was in pain?

In the long hours, shadowy pictures like double-exposure snapshots drifted before her: the grimy, gray faces of the men and women from the cannery. Those who could walk and speak and give their names, and the silent stretcher cases. The man with the severed artery. The blood-stained tourniquet. The strong young mother coming to give blood. The hungry baby.

And Miss Johnson's compassionate eyes as she leaned over the woman with the fuzzy hair. Had Miss Johnson whispered her name? *Helene.* The homely, pain-distorted face was not burned—but the arms and hands . . .

Was the woman still alive? *Helene* . . . Kathy frowned in the darkness, trying to remember where she had seen that name. The name—and the face, too, a vaguely familiar face.

The pain pounded steadily at her head. This was what it meant to be a patient. Nights were bad. She must remember that it helped if a nurse looked in now and then. "But we're always so busy. There's so little time—" she murmured drowsily. Then with a flash her mind went back to the disaster in First Aid. The figure on the stretcher was—she was sure it was—Mrs. Stein!

She fell at last into a deep, healing sleep that lasted until dawn. When she awoke, Kelley was nodding in a chair by the bed.

"Hi." Kelley straightened up. "Want anything?"

Kathy gestured for her to come closer. "Mrs. Stein is in the hospital. She was working in the cannery."

Kelley frowned. "You just dreamed it," she said in a professionally soothing voice. "You talked about her in your sleep."

"They ought to be told in the office. And the police should know. I didn't know her without the wig—and her eyes were closed. But I'm sure that's who it was. She's dreadfully burned."

"I wouldn't bother about it, Martin. Go back to sleep," Kelley said. She didn't like to see Kathy excite herself, since absolute quiet the first day or two made a great difference in recovery from concussion. She busied herself straightening the bedclothes, giving Kathy a sip of water through a glass straw, rubbing her arms with long soothing gestures, doing all the little things that she could think of to make a patient physically comfortable.

"She looked so pitiful lying on that stretcher—Mrs. Stein, I mean," Kathy said in a feverish voice. "But we have to let the police know about her being here, don't we? *If she is alive.*"

"Don't think about anything, now," Kelley answered firmly. "Mrs. Marcelene Thomas and her locket are just not worth it."

"I have to tell—on account of Mary. She'll be cleared. I'm not just imagining things, Jonesy. I'm sure it was Mrs. Stein on that stretcher. Miss Johnson spoke to her—called her Helene. That was the name on my team list—Mrs. Helene Stein."

Long after Kathy had dropped off to sleep again, Kelley turned the problem of Mrs. Stein around in her own mind. She had never worked with the woman, but Kathy's description—the wig, the withdrawn eyes—made a gloomy portrait. Something out of Hogarth, Kelley thought with her artist's eye. She believed that Mrs. Stein was probably guilty of taking the locket. She had been in Surgery before coming to Second West. Miss Johnson would have recognized her. Maybe Kathy wasn't just having fever dreams. Maybe the woman really had been brought to the hospital. Anyway, it was worth checking. But there wasn't any hurry. If the woman was burned as badly as Kathy said, she'd have to have skin grafts. She'd be in the hospital for a long time. The important thing now was to keep Kathy quiet long enough for the blood clot to absorb.

• • •

Five days later, Dr. Bowen stuck his head in Kathy's door.

"You've seen the X rays?" Kathy asked.

Bowen nodded. "You were lucky," he said. "The concussion is milder than I thought, the blood clot absorbing nicely. No sign of fracture."

"Martin luck," Kathy chuckled. "May I sit up? I'd like to look at my callers instead of at the cracks in the ceiling. I feel wonderful. Why don't you dismiss me, Doctor, in time for the Senior Show tonight?"

"Isn't that just like a nurse? They're a doctor's worst patients. You tell 'em they're going to live and right away they want to hop out of bed and go dancing. I'll send somebody to get rid of those ice packs and raise your bed and give you some pillows. I'll be back later to have a look at the lesion on your scalp."

When Dr. Bowen came by on his afternoon rounds, Kathy's parents and her brother Nick had arrived. Her father was sitting on the edge of a chair, his huge hands spread over his knees.

"Doctor!" He lumbered to his feet and the fragile chair fell backward with a crash. "You took good care of our little girl!"

"Five feet eight, Papa. Remember?"

"Your father is speaking relatively, Miss Martin," Dr. Bowen said. "That's a pretty bed jacket you have on."

"Linda Garfield's best," Kathy answered.

"I wondered. Didn't think it was quite your style."

Miss Simpson, the R.N. in attendance, stood disapproving in the doorway. Kathy knew how she felt. If nurses had their way, doctors would confine their conversation to giving necessary orders.

It was different when you were a patient. She was enjoying herself. And suddenly she realized that the doctor wasn't wasting time. He was studying her voice and her gestures. He seemed pleased to find her able to laugh and joke.

"She's coming along nicely, Mrs. Martin," he said. "But I think we'll keep her here a few days longer. Rest and quiet are what she needs."

Mrs. Martin nodded. "We won't stay long. We just drove up to see for ourselves how Kathy was—my husband and Nick and I. Our little Johnny came along, too, but they wouldn't let him upstairs. He's waiting in the lounge."

Just then through the window came a sound that was something between the roar of an elephant and the squeaking of a brake. It was followed by laborious notes on an accordion.

"That's Johnny!" Kathy explained cheerfully. "And the tune is *Happy Birthday*. It's the only one he knows."

It was almost midnight before Kathy's next visitors tiptoed in. Gail and Matt had slipped by the vigilant night nurse to tell Kathy about the Senior Show—a radiant Gail, with a vase of red roses clutched in her hands.

"The class sent them to me, just for writing the show —and Matt wrote half of it. Your skit was the hit of the piece, even if you couldn't be in it. Anyway, the flowers belong to you."

Matt and Gail set the vase on the bureau and left as quietly as they had come. Kathy put herself to sleep composing a letter of thanks to her classmates and wondering how she could press red roses into her scrapbook.

She had forgotten most of her fine phrases by morning, but began the letter again—this time with pen and paper.

To the Senior class:
You have no idea how terrific you are, or how pleasant you've made my "vacation" as a patient.

Let me make a list of all the people I'm grateful to— with student nurses at the very top. Here goes:

Student nurses

Doctors: (mine and others)

Head nurses: (the same gals who make out those awful reports about us turn into "good guys" when they think you're in trouble)

Instructors—they visit once or twice a day

Are you bored? I've just started!

Aides: If you've ever wondered, the patients couldn't do without 'em

Maids: They dusted the bureau three times today just to smell Gail's red roses

Ward Clerks: They bring "get well" cards

Tray girls: They bring food. They bring lots and take empty plates away

Orderlies: They look in to cheer me up every time they pass my door

Patients: The ambulatories come in to exchange symptoms, and tomorrow or the next day Doc says I can return their visits

Our housemother: Merriweather came, looking scared, and left the same way

Special gratitude to all you Seniors—one, two, three, take a bow!

In a department all her own: Kelley, who sat up with me that long first night and let me worry out loud

I love you all

Well, I guess this letter makes me a full-fledged registered CB (cornball).

Kathy signed her name hurriedly and stuck the letter under her pillow as she heard familiar footsteps in the hall. Kelley and Yo stopped by every afternoon on their way to the mental hospital. They talked mental health so much that Kathy felt she was taking an extra course without credit.

Today, however, both girls were rather quiet. Kelley prowled about the room moving objects aimlessly from one place to another, and Yo kept peering around the screen that separated Kathy from her roommate. The roommate was a young girl with mononucleosis. She was very quiet and apparently quite ill.

"She's asleep," Yo announced after a fast look around the screen. "Do you mind if I close the door?"

"What's the pitch?" Kathy was curious.

"It's Jonesy's story."

"You might not remember, Kathy," Kelley began, "that

first night when you were kind of restless—"

"I remember," Kathy said grimly. "You thought I was out of my mind when I said Mrs. Stein was one of the disaster victims and was somewhere in the hospital."

"Not out of your mind—just mixing up bad dreams with reality. But it's true. She *is* here—in the new wing on Third East. Garfield has been taking care of her AM shift. Cranshaw's on duty in the ward, too. Stein will have to have skin grafts. She'll be here a couple of months."

"Do they know in the office that Mrs. Stein, patient, is the same party as Mrs. Stein, ex-aide?"

"There's no hurry," Yo said. "The poor thing can't stand up or even turn over in bed without help. Cranshaw is waiting for you to make the report. You're the team leader. All you have to do is tell the superintendent, and then it's out of your hands. You see that, don't you, Martin?"

"And the mystery of the stolen locket is solved," Kathy said.

But her voice didn't have the lilt to it that Kelley had expected. "What's wrong with that plan?"

"Nothing," Kathy answered slowly. "At least I don't think there is. Certainly she had a good chance to steal the locket—but so did the rest of us."

"Nobody else ran away and hid the moment she was questioned," Kelley said.

"Working nights in a cannery isn't exactly running away," Kathy said, "though you could drop out of sight that way and wait until the police and the insurance company stopped looking for the jewelry. I suppose that's the way a thief might reason. I was just thinking about the little girl—her daughter. I was wondering if Miss Johnson knows who's taking care of the girl. And how much does Miss Johnson know? My head is aching a little. Let's talk some more tomorrow."

Next day Kathy was allowed to walk up and down the hall in bathrobe and slippers.

"Take it easy, Miss Martin," Tillie said, dashing by with an instrument tray.

Take it easy! Kathy shook her head ruefully. Her legs, unaccustomed to exercise, felt like lead. She couldn't have run if she'd had to. But she had a reason for lingering in the corridor. She was waiting for a moment when no one was around. The moment came, finally, when she was alone and conveniently near the elevator. She pressed the button, slipped through the doors as soon as they were half open, pressed another button for the third floor and a few moments later was knocking on the door of Miss Johnson's cubbyhole of an office.

"It's all right, my being out of bed," she said. "I'm going to be dismissed tomorrow. But I had to see you about Mrs. Stein and the thing that happened in September."

"I don't understand." Miss Johnson looked bewildered.

Kathy explained about the locket. "Mrs. Thomas accused Mary Cranshaw, you see. And then Stein ran away. I was the team leader." Kathy leaned against the door.

The room was moving up and down like waves on the ocean. "What would happen to her daughter if Mrs. Stein got arrested?"

"You'd better come in and sit down, Miss Martin," Alice Johnson said and helped Kathy to a chair. "I'm going to break the code of nursing ethics and tell you what I know about Helene Stein."

CHAPTER X

Miss Johnson's Story

Miss Johnson wasted no words. "I have known Helene Stein for many years," she began. "I first met her when I was a student nurse in Philadelphia, soon after World War II. That was 1947—ancient history to you. I was on Senior Service in the Maternity Ward, caring for the new mothers. Most of them were happy—it was the happiest place in the hospital.

"This one woman ought to have been happy: her husband came every day; the baby was a fine, pretty little thing, perfectly normal. But here was this mother, just lying there, refusing to talk. When I first brought the baby to her, she wouldn't touch it. Just stared at the child and at me. She kept a big shawl around her head. I knew why—she had hardly any hair, just a soft fuzz. I put the baby in her arms and the ends of the shawl folded round it. When I went to take the baby away, she held it so tight I had to tell her to be careful.

"Well, you know how it is. When you're a student nurse, you feel mighty close to your patients. So one day I just stayed on after my shift. I didn't talk, just stayed

91

around. After a little, this woman opened up, speaking in some kind of foreign accent that was hard for me to understand.

"Helene Stein had come from a town on the border between Poland and Germany. It's Polish now, but was German when she grew up. She'd been a trained nurse. Her husband was a cattle farmer. When Hitler came along, the Steins had been married about two years. They had a son, just a few months old.

"Uniformed officials came with 'Heil Hitlers' and lots of questions. Why wasn't Stein in the army? Was he loyal to Hitler? Was it true his wife was not Jewish? Questions and more questions. And one day, the questioners took her husband away. Nazi soldiers moved onto the farm. They watched her all the time. About 1943 Helene and the boy were taken to a concentration camp. Somehow they managed to survive, for two long years. During that time she had typhoid fever and lost her hair. The little boy had typhoid, too—and he died.

"Then in the spring of 1945, she told me, rumors began flying around the camp. The Nazis were losing the war. More rumors said that the Americans were moving east, the Russians were coming west to join them. The Storm Troopers in charge of the camp were loading people in carts and carrying them away—rumor said, to be shot. First the men, then the women and children.

"It was mid-April of '45 when they began loading up the death carts in Helene's section of the camp. The women knew why. Helene knew why. She didn't care. Her husband was gone. Her son was dead. She was ready.

"The Nazi soldiers lined them up in the woods and began shooting. But somehow—by some miracle—six or seven of the women in the middle of the line were simply missed. Helene was one of these. There was no thought, no plan of escape. They just broke out of the line and ran into the trees. The soldiers didn't even bother to follow them. They made their way to a farmhouse and hid there. A few days later, American soldiers found them and took them to a displaced-persons' camp. There they were slowly brought back to health."

Kathy hadn't stirred. She leaned forward now. "Th_ _ she came to America?"

"Months later, through the Red Cross, Helen Stein heard that her husband had also escaped. They were reunited and brought to this country. And this new baby, Elena, was born here. But Helene couldn't believe the baby was safe, couldn't believe that this child would grow up secure and free.

"I kept in touch with her and helped her with the baby. I even got her to buy a wig. We became good friends. Then I moved out here and lost touch with her until about three years ago.

"She looked me up in San Mateo, where I live. Her husband had died and she didn't know what to do. She had withdrawn into herself, terrified like that first time I knew her. Elena, the little girl, was nine. Helene was afraid to let her out of her sight. The child had never even been allowed to walk to school alone.

"I tried to persuade Mrs. Stein to go back into nursing. She was afraid to—afraid she'd get separated from her daughter. Finally, I persuaded her to get some psychiatric help. I kept the child. After about a year in the mental hospital, Helene was willing to go to work as an aide here.

"You've seen for yourself how difficult it is for her to make friends. But things seemed to be going along smoothly, until she disappeared again—she and Elena."

"It was that locket," Kathy burst out. "Mrs. Thomas accused Mary Cranshaw of stealing it—and I was sure that Mary wasn't guilty. And Mrs. Stein was on my team and had just as much opportunity to take the locket as Mary did—and I started asking her questions. Then the insurance men came and she ran away—so we all decided she was guilty. I was her team leader and I ought to have defended her, but I was glad to have an outsider to blame!"

"You couldn't have shielded her, Martin. But I might have, if I had heard anything about it. She just left her apartment with no explanation to the landlady or anybody. And I didn't see her again until the night of the explosion. I hardly recognized her without the wig—and she was burned so badly."

"Why did she hide if she hadn't stolen the locket, Miss Johnson?"

"Helene wouldn't take a piece of bread if she were starving," Miss Johnson said gravely. "I think questioning by any kind of officials reminded her of the past and made her afraid she'd be separated from Elena."

"May I tell Mrs. Stein's story to my roommates and a couple of others?" Kathy asked. "I'm so glad she didn't steal the locket. And I feel terrible about having suspected her."

"It happened so long ago that telling it can hurt no one. I'm hoping when Helene gets out of the hospital she'll enroll in a refresher course in nursing and do the work she's trained for. But that's for the future. Just now I want *you* to go back to bed. This sort of thing is the worst kind of therapy for a concussion case."

"You're wrong, Miss Johnson!" Kathy hadn't felt so light-hearted since last September. "I'll be good, thoug', and crawl back under the blankets."

She met Jenny at the elevator, waiting to go down for her coffee break.

"Skip the coffee, Ramirez," Kathy said. "Come tuck me in bed. I've got something to tell you."

Jenny listened to Miss Johnson's story repeated almost word for word. "So you see, every single thing we thought about Mrs. Stein was wrong," Kathy finished, and snuggled down in her pillows with a happy sigh.

"That's true." Jenny's eyes were filled with tears. "Still, it doesn't follow that she'll be willing to come back to the hospital. It's not enough, Kathy, that we don't believe her guilty any longer. She's got to be proved inno-cent so she has nothing to fear. The only way to do that is to find the locket."

Kathy bounced up again. "Or find the real thief, Ra-mirez! The Do-It-Yourself Detective Agency just opened its office for business again."

CHAPTER XI

Linda Flips

"What do you mean, you don't know where she is?"

"Just exactly that, Jim. I don't know." Kathy looked with some irritation at the belligerent young man standing in the doorway of the Merriweather house. She had known Jim Telford since kindergarten days. During freshman year at San Tomás, she had been delighted to watch his growing friendship with Linda. But Jim and Linda had been going steady for two years now, and Kathy resented Jim's accusing voice. As if she had nothing to do but keep track of his girl!

Jim's belligerence melted away under her steady gaze. "I'm sorry, Kath. I was surprised, that's all . . . I mean, this is my last free weekend before finals—"

"And Linda usually spends Saturday afternoon watching for you out of the third-floor tower, like the princess in the fairy tale. Come in, spoiled prince, and have a Coke. Matt's here, too, so you won't be overwhelmed by nurses," she said over her shoulder as Jim followed her down the long hall to the kitchen.

Kathy had been back in uniform for a week. With the

semester nearing its end, with the extra patient load since the cannery disaster, and with every outside moment taken up by meetings of the Do-It-Yourself Detective Agency, there had hardly been time to worry about Linda's unexplained absences.

Linda's strange behavior had begun the day Kathy was dismissed as a patient from the hospital. The girls were sitting on the floor around her bed, planning their campaign to trace the lost locket. Linda had listened eagerly at first. Then a faraway look had come into her eyes. "I know a better thing to do," she had announced, "than making lists of suspects."

For the first few days, Gail had tried to get Linda to divulge her idea or at least her whereabouts—as one roommate to another. But Linda, usually so willing and eager to talk, wouldn't open her mouth. At last, even Gail had stopped asking questions. By Saturday, her absence had come to seem natural—until Jim Telford arrived.

"Move some pieces, Sherlock Henderson," Kathy said. "You've got so many lists there isn't room for Jim to set down his Coke."

Gail barely looked up as she shoved a handful of papers to the center of the table. "Look, Kathy. Matt's got a new proposal. Suppose the old lady stole her own locket. I mean, suppose she needed the insurance money or something."

"Oh, no," Kathy said firmly. "No, not unless she's an

old Shakespearean actress, and then she'd have had to rehearse for a year. No, Mrs. Thomas wanted that locket back. There's no doubt about that."

Christopher Matthews leaned back in his chair. "Okay," he said with a twinkle. "She's an old Shakespearean actress. Distant cousin of the Barrymores."

"Wait a minute, Matt," Jim Telford broke in. "I hate to seem ignorant, but would somebody mind telling me what this is all about?"

Kathy started a long explanation, which Gail kept interrupting by handing Jim lists of names.

"Here's a list of all the people who were in the patient's room the day the locket was lost. Everybody from the doctor and nurses to the cleaning woman and the tray girl. There weren't any outside visitors," Gail said.

Kathy kept talking steadily. "We were dead wrong about Mrs. Stein. She's no longer on the list of suspects, but Jenny doesn't think she'll come back to nursing unless we can prove her innocence. We've got to find the thief—"

"Or the locket," Gail said, fluttering another sheet of paper under Jim's eyes. "Here are the questions the insurance people asked."

"Whoa!"

"That's what you get for going off to Berkeley," Matt laughed. "You have to enter when the curtain goes up to understand the goings-on of San Tomás nurses."

"Well, all I really wanted to know is where my girl has disappeared to," Jim said. "Any clues to that?"

The front door slammed and they all stopped to listen. But the laughter and the tramping footsteps were not Linda's.

"Martin? Where are you?" Kelley called. "We've found Linda—only you'll never believe where!"

Yo and Jenny followed Kelley into the kitchen. They stopped short at the sight of Jim.

"Where is she? What's she up to?" Jim looked worried.

"Well," Kelley said, "it seems she took a notion that she, single-handed, was going to earn enough money to put Mrs. Stein through a refresher course so she could come back to San Tomás as an R.N., in one of those fancy foreign caps."

"So she started studying the want ads," Yo picked up, as Kelley stopped for breath. "And she found an ad for an afternoon—and weekend—job."

"We were walking by that new supermarket on Tenth Street," Jenny said, "and they had a promotion stunt going on. For some new kind of pancake mix. *'Instant Hotcakes,'* this voice announced over the loudspeaker. *'Add nothing but water. Taste just like the ones Grandma used to make.'* They were offering free samples, and there was a crowd around the window.

"So we went over to see what was going on—Jonesy being hungry, as usual. And there in the window, wearing the biggest chef's cap you ever saw, was Linda!"

"Miss Instant Hotcakes, you mean," Yo said. "Flipping pancakes as fast as she could. You should have seen her face when she saw us! We went in and waited till she could take a break, and she confessed all. She gets fifty cents an hour and a half-cent commission on every box sold!"

"All she needs to sell," Kelley added, "is fifty thousand boxes or so. And the sample pancakes taste *exactly* as advertised. Just like some that Grandma made—and preserved for all these years!"

"But she's determined to go on with it. She wouldn't quit, even after we reminded her that finals were just three weeks off." Yo shook her head.

"What Linda needs," said Jim thoughtfully, "is a *really* la. e crowd of customers. May I use the phone, Kathy?"

. i hour later, an impressive crowd appeared at the Ten i Street Supermarket. If there seemed to be an unusual number of young men, no one commented on the fact. jim had mustered a small army of ex-classmates and these, with the five student nurses, converged on the window marked "New. Different. INSTANT Hotcakes."

For a while, Miss Instant Hotcakes (the name was on the cap) was unaware of her enlarged audience. Kathy and Gail, Matt and Jim watched entranced. Like an automaton, Linda mixed batter, poured batter, and flipped neat, round hotcakes. A stout man, standing next to Jim, seemed much impressed. "Believe I'll get a box," he said.

Jim didn't seem to hear. Instead, he tapped firmly on

the window. Miss Instant Hotcakes glanced up as she began to pour a new batch of batter.

Her hand froze in mid-air. Her eyes seemed to get larger and larger as they moved from one familiar face to another. The single, enormous hotcake on the griddle also grew larger. Miss Hotcakes looked down, then up again. Carefully, she took the pancake turner in hand. Deliberately, she lifted the gooey mass—and with one deft stroke flipped it right against the big store window.

"Oh, no!" Yo pinched Kathy's arm. "Here comes the boss. Poor Linda isn't going to get a chance to quit. She's fired!"

"It's Jim I'm worried about, not Linda," Kathy glanced at her watch. "He's only got five hours and fifteen minutes before midnight to make Linda believe that he is very sympathetic and was just trying to be helpful!"

CHAPTER XII

Kathy Breaks a Date

"Well, didn't it rain, children,
  Didn't it rain?"

"It did, indeed, but do you have to sound so cheerful about it, Miss Mahalia Jackson Nakayama?" Kathy groaned, as she pulled rubber boots over her white shoes.

January at the residence on South Maple was a month of long hours and short tempers. Semester finals were just around the corner. That meant study in every spare moment. Nobody got to bed on time, and it was still pitch dark when the girls left for hospital duty at 6:30 in the morning. And it rained. Storms blew in from the Pacific, up the coast from Mexico and down the coast from Washington. The valley turned from dusty brown to dingy gray, and the girls sloshed through puddles from South Maple to the hospital, from the hospital to the muddy college campus—growling at themselves, at each other, and particularly at California's liquid sunshine. Only Yo took the weather completely in stride.

"It's because of the strawberries," she said a little apologetically. Yo watched the "inches of rainfall" column in the daily paper with almost as much interest as she did the column of mercury on her patient's thermometers.

"I know," said Kathy. "Apples need the rain too. But does it have to go on all day, every day?"

"Not to mention all night," Jenny put in. "I got up three times last night to turn off a dripping faucet that wasn't there. It was just the rain hitting the balcony."

"In the first place," said Yo, "this is only the third day in a row. Just Monday you were admiring the sunlight on the snow up on Mt. Hamilton. In the second place, San Tomás has the best climate—"

"Well, listen to the Chamber of Commerce," Kathy teased.

"—of any place in the world," Yo went on, ignoring the interruption. "And in the third place, unless I miss my guess, it'll be clear by lunchtime today. Look at the sky over there. It's got kind of a pinkish tinge."

The only pinkish tinge Kathy noticed during the morning on First Aid came from a spilled bottle of merthiolate. But by noon, Yo's prediction turned out to be true.

Kathy's spirits brightened along with the weather, and in a burst of efficiency she managed to complete her records half an hour before her shift ended. Casting only one wistful glance at a pile of magazines, she took out *The Legal Aspects of Nursing*, propped it up on the counter, and went to work.

"Is this First Aid? Anybody here?"

Kathy looked up in surprise. She hadn't thought she was invisible. Then she understood. The young man standing in the doorway had as a companion a large, solemn-eyed German shepherd, heavily harnessed—a Seeing Eye dog.

"Right here. May I help you?"

Even before she spoke, the visitor began limping toward the desk. Mid-twenties, Kathy guessed. About her own height, dark hair, deep-set blue eyes. Lined face. Lips compressed. Evidently in some pain.

Kathy repressed the natural instinct of the sighted to rush to the aid of the blind. Rather deliberately, she slipped from behind the counter.

"You've hurt your foot? Step over to this room, please."

The dog whimpered ever so softly as Kathy took the patient's arm.

"It's all right, Sandy. It wasn't your fault. You warned me to stay out of that mud."

"A puddle on the sidewalk?" Kathy asked. "Is that how you slipped?"

"No, I left the straight and narrow path—against my dog's advice." The young man settled himself in the chair and extended his muddy shoe. "Down the block, where that big old acacia tree is just showing yellow."

"But—" Kathy knew the tree. She'd noticed the first blooms when the sun came out at lunchtime, where yesterday there'd been only tight, wet buds. But how could a blind person tell?

" 'I cannot see what flowers are at my feet, nor what soft incense wafts the boughs,' " the young man quoted lightly. "But I've a nose and I can smell. Still, I needn't have broken the Fifth Commandment."

Kathy mumbled the Ten Commandments to herself as she counted on her fingers. "Thou shalt not covet," she announced triumphantly. "You tried to pick a branch and slipped in the mud."

She took a quick glance at the ankle. Definite swelling. "I think a doctor had better see this. Who is your doctor?"

"Dr. Ash. But I don't need him for a twisted ankle."

Dr. Ash, Kathy knew, was a heart man, a well-known specialist. She looked at the patient's face, and then turned her eyes away again with the rather disconcerting feeling that he not only could see, but could read her mind.

"I'll call Ash," she said. "He'll probably want the resident physician to have a look at you. May I have your name, please?"

"Gordon McKinlay."

Kathy remembered having heard the name—perhaps from Matt. He'd talked about a blind graduate student in his Chaucer class at State.

By the time she reached Dr. Ash and then called for Dr. Brier, the resident, it was three o'clock. The PM nurse came on duty.

Kathy handed over the day's records. "I'll finish up the patient in Room A," she said. "That'll leave you free."

"Who've you got in there? A good-looking young fellow?" The PM nurse was an old-timer whose idea of fun was to tease the students.

Unreasonably, Kathy found herself blushing. She laid Gordon McKinlay's card on the desk and followed Dr. Brier into Room A.

The patient thrust out his swollen foot.

"A tensor bandage should do it," Brier said after a brief examination. "X ray won't be necessary."

Gordon talked soothingly to the dog as Kathy slowly wound the bandage. She was trying to think of a tactful way to make sure that the patient got safely to wherever he was going.

"Can I call a taxi for you?" she said when she had managed, with some difficulty, to get the shoe back on and loosely tied. "Were you going to class? You are a student at State, aren't you? Or maybe you'd want to go home."

"Home is only a block and a half away. Sandy and I can manage, thank you."

Before Kathy could explain that she was going in his direction anyway, he was gone. A wallet lay on the chair. It had fallen from his jacket, no doubt. Kathy snatched up her cape and ran after him.

They strolled down the street together.

"It smells like spring," he said.

"Doesn't it?" Kathy sniffed audibly. "Makes me hungry for the country. I'd like to get out and walk and walk and walk."

"I know," the young man answered. "It's spring walking fever. I get it, too. So did Chaucer." He raised his head and took a breath, like a singer, and began to recite:

> *"When that April with his showers sweet*
> *The drought of March hath pierced to the root,*
> *And small birds make melody*
> *That sleep all night with open eye,*
> *Then all folk long to go on pilgrimage."*

Kathy recognized the opening lines of Chaucer's Canterbury Tales, but she had never heard them spoken aloud before.

"Go on pilgrimage," she repeated after him, enchanted. "Only it's not April, but January."

"And California, not England—and not the fourteenth century," Gordon agreed. "But pilgrimages are for everyone and for all time. Poets and musicians are forever trying to catch the feel of spring walking fever. Maybe, today, jazz says it best?"

The last was a question, not a statement. Kathy didn't know how to answer. She didn't know much about jazz, except that it was something to dance to with Steve Kovak. She glanced sideways at the young man keeping pace with her slow stride. A block and a half wasn't very long to get acquainted. He talked about music so knowingly. He must be a music major.

"No," he said in answer to her direct question, "I took my B.A. in English. Now I'm working in education. Eventually, I'd like to teach. Right now, I'm getting ready for my oral examination. I've finished my master's thesis on 'Sound Perception in Language Learning Among the Blind.'"

"Wow! That's over my head."

Gordon laughed. "Then it must be over mine, too. We seem to be about the same height." He had stopped in front of a good-sized stucco house, newer than most on the block. "Here's where I live."

A plump, graying-blond woman ran down the steps from the porch, concern written on her face. She checked herself midway down the walk, and rearranged her features in a careful smile.

"Hello, Mother," Gordon said quickly, reassuringly, suddenly remembering that he was limping and was accompanied by a stranger in nurse's uniform. "I gave my ankle a twist. Had it bound up at First Aid. It's quite all right."

He turned to Kathy. "This is my mother, Miss—" He stopped. "Stupid of me. We were so busy talking I forgot to ask your name."

"Kathy Martin. How do you do, Mrs. McKinlay. Your son is quite correct. He is all right. I just happened to be on my way to the Nursing School residence."

Mrs. McKinlay put out her hand. "I wasn't worried," she said. "Won't you come in and have a cup of tea?"

"Good idea," Gordon seconded with enthusiasm. "Just what the doctor ordered."

The front door opened directly into a huge low-ceilinged living room. "As big as a three-room apartment," Kathy said to herself. In the fireplace at one end of the room a cheerful fire was burning. A chair was drawn up by the fire. Beside it was a table piled with books printed in Braille. There were also a remote-control switch for the radio and a dish of fudge.

"Gordon's domain," Mrs. McKinlay said.

Opposite, on a coffee table in front of a couch, was a bowl of sweet-smelling daphne, an open book of Mother Goose rhymes, stiff sheets of paper and a Braille punch.

"My busy-work," the older woman explained, and put the pages of Braille aside. "For the second-graders in the school for the blind."

"What a lovely room!" Kathy explored with her eyes. One whole wall of books. A twelve-string guitar leaning against an upright piano. A chess table under the window, with the pieces set up. Photographs of Gordon on the walls: Gordon in cap and gown; Gordon on the deck of a ship; Gordon, a boy of nine or ten, with a German shepherd crouching at his feet.

"Are you admiring the picture of Star?" Gordon asked. "She was my first Seeing Eye dog. I got her a year after my sight went bad."

For the moment, Kathy had forgotten that he was blind.

"If your ankle is swollen, hadn't you better take your shoe off?" Mrs. McKinlay asked. "I'll go put on water for tea."

In a moment, Gordon was back in moccasins. He drew up a third chair before the fire and held it for Kathy to sit down.

"You're tall, a nurse . . ."

"Student nurse," she corrected.

"And your name is Kathy Martin. What else?"

"What else is there? I'm a country girl with no accomplishments."

"But you have a taste for going on pilgrimages," Gordon reminded her. "Blond or brunette?" he persisted.

"Chestnut brown curls and very pretty," Gordon's mother said, coming in with the tea tray.

Kathy watched Mrs. McKinlay's skillful arrangement of the tea things. How eager she was to give her son a normal life!

After tea, Kathy got up to go. Mrs. McKinlay took her to the door and thanked her for stopping by. "It's good for Gordon to have young people around him, don't you think?"

Strains of music came from the room. "Like liquid gold," Kathy thought. She stopped, her hand on the doorknob. "What is that piece they're playing on the radio?"

Mrs. McKinlay smiled. "It's a melody from Delius' *On Hearing the First Cuckoo in Spring*, but it's not the radio. It's Gordon at the piano."

Kathy spent the two blocks to Maple Street thinking about Gordon McKinlay. Courage, a sense of humor, talent—he was a remarkable person. A person she'd like to know better. She found herself dreaming up absurd ways to see Gordon McKinlay again.

But, as it happened, she didn't need any of her invented excuses. At noon the next day, he appeared at the door of First Aid.

"I thought my bandage might be a little loose," he explained.

"Looks in perfect shape to me," Kathy said in her most professional manner.

"Of course it is," Gordon grinned, not at all abashed. "I thought I should have a professional reason for coming by. I really wanted to say that a few friends are coming over this evening to sing folk songs. Thought you might like to join us."

"I can't carry a tune," Kathy said. "But I'd love to come."

She got home from the folk-song evening just as the PM shift was over, and insisted that Jenny get out her guitar and teach her the chorus of *Careless Love*. "Just in case I get invited to the McKinlays again," she said, "I won't feel like such a dope."

Gordon followed the evening of folk singing with an invitation to the jazz festival at college. Almost every day he and Sandy were waiting outside the door of First Aid when she came off duty at three o'clock.

Her classmates saw little of Kathy, but it was exam time and nobody had much time to notice anyone else. Gordon had exams, too. And the rains set in again. For a couple of days she heard nothing from him.

Then his mother telephoned. Would Kathy care to go on a family picnic to Big Basin on Sunday, if the weather permitted? "Gordon's father is home for the weekend. He has to travel around so much that we declare a family celebration whenever he's home."

The Big Basin State Park was only twenty-five or thirty miles away from San Tomás, but off the main-traveled roads. The day of the picnic was warm and sunny, but the lofty branches of the giant redwoods made a green twilight. There was little undergrowth—only a few tall ferns.

Not many visitors came into the forest at this season. The squirrels and deer had it almost to themselves.

"Except for us." Kathy was blissful. When lunch was over, Mr. McKinlay declared that he was going to take a nap. His wife opened the novel she had brought.

"You two might as well have stayed home by the fire," Gordon teased. "I want to explore. I keep hearing the sound of a running brook."

"It must be down there," Kathy said, pointing to a distant spot where the sun managed to filter through. "Where willows grow, there's bound to be water."

They found a brook and a waterfall, and red and yellow columbine growing in the crevices of huge boulders.

All around them were the thousand-year-old trees, red-barked and majestic.

"Be my eyes," Gordon said. "You know so much more about nature than I do."

"I told you the first day we met that I was a country girl." Kathy's hand was on Gordon's arm, and as they threaded their way downstream she guided him, lightly, skillfully. She was very happy.

"Would you come to my graduation?" Gordon asked. "I have two tickets and Father is off to London."

"Oh, Gordon, I'd love to. But—" Kathy had a holiday on Friday. It would be her long weekend of the winter. Since she couldn't come home for Christmas, Steve had made plans with his cousin and her husband. The four of them would go to Yosemite Friday and Saturday to see the snow. She had a post card on her desk reminding her. Steve had drawn a snowman, and simply written inside a red circle: "X marks the day."

"If you've got something else to do, Kathy," Gordon said, "don't give it a second thought. I suppose it's juvenile to think so much of getting a degree. But when it comes the hard way—well, I'm twenty-seven, you know. I lost some time in school getting used to being blind—and there was the year Dr. Ash took me out of college and stuck me in bed. Since then, with my little nitro pills—"

"I wondered about your heart," Kathy said, "when you mentioned that Ash was your doctor."

"It was the defect in the heart that caused my eyes to go," Gordon explained. "Let's forget it. Don't know how I got started on such a dull subject. Listen to that blue jay protesting."

"Not even the sky is as heavenly blue as the California jay," Kathy responded. "Gordon—it'll be all right about graduation. I—I couldn't bear to miss it. I'll phone and break my date as soon as we get home."

"Steve will understand," she said to herself. "Gordon needs me."

CHAPTER XIII

"Be My Eyes"

"Did Martin have a whirl at Yosemite?" Gail asked as she and Kelley stood in line halfway down the block from the Administration Building. They had come straight from their morning shift at the hospital to register for the spring semester at State. "I haven't seen her since the weekend."

"She didn't go."

"That's too bad." Gail moved a few feet forward in the line, to a puddle six inches deep. "What happened? Did Steve have a fire in this weather?"

Kelley shook her head. "No, Kathy stood Steve up to go to Gordon McKinlay's graduation. Her head's in the clouds. I'm worried about her. Can't we do something?"

"Better not," Gail advised. "Let Nature take its course. Besides, Matt says Gordon's an extraordinary person."

"I don't doubt it," Kelley answered gloomily. "But Steve Kovak is the right man for Kathy. I've half a mind to write him that he'd better dash up here and put out the smoldering blaze."

Spring had come to San Tomás for good. "Be my

eyes," Gordon had said to Kathy that day in the red-woods. For two weekends she led him on "pilgrimages" through the procession of orchards blossoming from the first almonds and plums to the pink clouds of apricots.

She helped him see not only the blossoms but the patterns of the orchards, the different forms of the trees, the gnarled ruggedness of the stubby apricots, the up-reaching, delicate branches of the almond trees, the purple of young cabbages, the silver blue of artichokes, and the color of the mustard and the poppies—both yellow, but with a difference. When she was at a loss for words, Gordon could find them in a line of the poetry with which his mind was richly stored.

Those country tramps together were for the weekends only. Walking across campus or along the streets to the hospital, Kathy often tried closing her eyes to the brilliant sunshine to test how many signs of spring she could detect through the sense of sound or of touch alone.

She tried to describe the sensation to Steve in a letter, but gave it up as a bad job. That worried her, because she'd always enjoyed new experiences twice over when she shared them with Steve. She'd be glad, she said to herself, when Gordon and Steve knew each other. Maybe they could all ride down next weekend to see the apple blossoms at the ranch.

"It's a beautiful spring, isn't it?" she said one day early in March to the Junior circulating nurse who came over to tie the string of her apron and help her on with her gloves. It was Kathy's second operation of the day as scrub nurse.

"I wouldn't know," the girl answered. "I just keep my nose in my pathology book. How on earth did you Seniors ever memorize all those blood types? Don't try to answer. Turn around and hold your hands out straight while I tie your strings."

Kathy let her thoughts wander. The operation scheduled was an appendectomy. The one before had been to put pins in a fractured hip. Funny how calmly you came to take routine jobs in surgery. Not the unusual ones, of course—like Mrs. Stein's first skin graft yesterday. Four hours. Miss Johnson had been scrub nurse. Kathy, as team leader, had circulated, with Cranshaw to help. Exhausting. But what a beautiful job!

She had been so excited about it that she'd stopped on the way home to tell Gordon . . . and then she'd had to tell him the whole story about Mrs. Stein's life and the awful mistake they'd made about the lost locket. So now there was a new member of the Do-It-Yourself Detective Agency. Gordon had insisted on being a part of the search. "*Ex officio*, with the inner eye, because Sandy and I can't go poking around the hospital," he said.

She'd ended up by staying too late and then getting up too early.

"Gloves, Martin," the Junior said. "Now your mask." She rushed off to open the door. The orderlies were bringing the patient in.

Dr. Smith was talking to the surgeon. Both were masked, and stiffly held out gloved hands.

Overhead, the loudspeaker was putting in a call. "Dr. Ash. Dr. Ash." *Ash.* Kathy's heart missed a beat. He was Gordon's doctor. You didn't hear him paged often. Mostly he came to the hospital on consultation.

"Doctor Stat, Doctor Stat to First Aid, please." Was it only her imagination, or had the call come through with a special urgency? "Dr. Ash, Dr. Ash . . ." A heart attack was always urgent. That's the way it would be if Gordon— "Dr. Stat. Dr. Stat to First Aid, please."

Kathy shivered. Then she took herself sternly in hand. The call for Dr. Ash and the emergency call probably had no connection at all.

"Ready, Martin," Dr. Smith said.

* * *

Kathy hurried out of the operating room when her duty was over. She had a coffee break coming. There'd be time to go down to check and put her mind at rest.

The elevator stopped at the second floor for a maid to wheel on a hamper of laundry. Impatiently, Kathy got out and walked down the long corridor and through the doors to Second West. If Gordon *had* been brought into the hospital with a heart attack, this is where he'd be.

"Kathy!" She felt no real surprise at hearing Mrs. Mc-Kinlay call her name. Gordon's mother was sitting at the West elevator, where families of patients often took up their vigil to waylay nurses coming along the corridor or doctors on their rounds. Mrs. McKinlay was quiet and composed. She had been through this often before.

Yes, she said, Gordon had had an attack about an hour ago. Fortunately, he had been at home, and the ambulance had come very promptly. He was getting oxygen. They'd located Dr. Ash. The doctor was with Gordon now.

"I asked about you, my dear," Mrs. McKinlay said. "I thought that if Gordon needed special nursing he'd like to have someone he knows. But they said at the desk that was impossible, on account of your being a student in training."

Kathy nodded dumbly. She didn't trust herself to speak. She walked on down the corridor. There was just one door with an OXYGEN—NO SMOKING sign. Below it, another sign: NO VISITORS. That would be Gordon's. If Dr. Ash was with him, she didn't dare go in. She went back to Mrs. McKinlay.

"I'm on duty upstairs," she said. "I'm in Surgery. I have to go now. I'll be back."

Four hours later, when Kathy was free, Second West was dark and still. The door of Gordon's room was almost closed. The signs were still there.

Kathy ignored the NO VISITORS sign, pushed the door open wide enough to slide through. A tiny, shaded lamp on the nightstand was the only light. The room was filled with the sound of Gordon's labored breathing, the soft hiss of the oxygen tank. The R.N. in the chair by the nightstand glanced up, then walked over to meet Kathy by the door.

"Is it all right if I see the patient for just a minute?" Kathy said softly. "I'm a friend of his."

"All right." The Special was one of the older nurses. Kathy couldn't remember her name, but they had worked together before. "I'll take a quick coffee break while you're with the patient. Orders are not to leave him alone."

"Kathy?" Gordon was conscious.

"Yes, Gordon." The oxygen tank was by the bed, the tubes in his nostrils.

"Are you really here?"

His voice was faint, far away, and his hands moved restlessly on the covers. She took one hand in both of hers and held it lightly. Then she put his hands back under the covers. She was still standing by the bed when the Special returned and nodded a dismissal.

Somehow she got home and let herself into the house. She wakened Kelley and told her about Gordon. Kelley was on AM duty on Gordon's floor. She'd be taking care of him tomorrow. "If there is a tomorrow," Kathy sobbed.

Kelley let her cry and promised to call if there was any change when she got to the hospital. Then she persuaded Kathy to go to bed. "Even if you don't sleep," she said.

But when Kelley tiptoed out the next morning, Kathy was sleeping. At noon she was on Second West.

Gordon was still on the critical list. His mother was in

the room, quietly watching, waiting. Dr. Ash had been in twice.

Kathy looked for Kelley. The question she couldn't bring herself to ask was in her eyes. Kelley gave her a look at the chart, which left the question still unanswered. Kathy went back and stayed in the room until time to go up to Surgery. She worked in a sort of trance, carefully repeating orders, forcing her hands to do the jobs that had to be done, trying not to hear the part of her that was asking over and over, "Is he going to die?"

Then, the next afternoon, there was a change. Kelley called at the Residence. "Out of immediate danger," the doctor had said.

Kathy's eyes were shining when she hurried down the hall. She had just a few minutes before her shift. Mrs. McKinlay met her at the door.

"He's sleeping, Kathy. Don't go in."

Kathy looked in surprise at the older woman. Her voice had sounded flat, almost cold. "My roommate told me that he's out of danger."

Mrs. McKinlay smiled wearily. "Yes, the news is wonderful. All his friends can be very happy. But this has been a bad one. We've always known—my husband and I—that Gordon could never be really well. We've tried to give him as rich a life as anyone could have . . ." Her voice trailed off.

Kathy had the feeling Mrs. McKinlay was about to say something more. But she just stood with her hand on the door knob, barring the way. Finally she said, "You're going to be late for work."

Kathy turned away, puzzled and somehow hurt. Of course, Mrs. McKinlay was tired, but it was more than that. It was as if she didn't want Kathy to see Gordon. Or—Kathy tried to brush away the thought—as if Gordon himself did not want to see her! "Maybe he told his mother to keep me out. Maybe, now that he is getting better, he doesn't need me any more."

At eleven that night Kathy started for home, but at the hospital door she turned, went upstairs again and stood irresolutely outside Gordon's door.

She didn't intend to go in, just to stand there a moment, perhaps to look in to assure herself that he was asleep.

Kathy pushed the door open a little wider and stopped. "Kathy?" Gordon was speaking in a perfectly normal voice. Heart patients were like that, Kathy said to herself. As soon as the attack passed, their strength returned. That was why it was so hard to keep them quiet while their heart muscles mended. "I've been listening for your footsteps."

"I'm here, Gordon—just long enough to say good night."

Softly Kathy tiptoed away. Gordon *did* want her and need her! She saw a life ahead dedicated to his service. A day or two of waiting was of no importance now.

When she opened the door of the Senior Residence,

the phone was ringing. "Long distance calling Miss Martin." *Long distance! That could mean something wrong at home.*

"This is Kathy Martin speaking," she said in a voice that trembled.

"Hi, Kathy!" It was Steve—Steve, whose last letter lay in her desk drawer, unanswered.

"Steve! Is anything wrong?"

"Everything's fine down here," he said. "Good news— I called earlier to tell you. Kelley said you'd be coming in about this time. I got that promotion I've been waiting for—head of the forest-fire division. No more twenty-four hours on, twenty-four hours off! Free weekends—except, of course, in emergencies. Thought we might celebrate by driving up to San Francisco for a show Saturday night."

"Oh Steve, it's wonderful—about your job, I mean. But I'm afraid Saturday won't be possible. There's a patient —Gordon McKinlay, the one I told you about. He's in the hospital, getting over a heart attack. He needs me. You understand, don't you, Steve?"

There was a long silence and then Steve's voice, sounding very far away: "I'm afraid I do understand. Good-by, Kathy."

"But, Steve!" Kathy heard the unmistakable click of the receiver. Steve was no longer on the line. If he had only listened, she could have explained about Gordon. Should she call back? Or would it be better to write?

Kathy turned away from the telephone. "Tomorrow," she promised herself, "I'll write Steve a letter." But she knew in her heart that it was a promise she would not keep.

•   •   •

Two days later, Mrs. McKinlay met Kathy in the hall.

"Gordon's sitting up in bed. Come in for a few minutes, Kathy. Sit with him while he has his lunch."

Gordon took her hand affectionately. "Look who's here," he said. "They've let me have Sandy."

The dog, still as a statue by the bed, moved just a little and put a paw against Kathy's knee.

"Sandy wants you to sit down and tell us what's going on in the world."

"Not today, Gordon. I have to go on duty now. But now that you're better, I'll come in my free time every day."

CHAPTER XIV

Mrs. McKinlay

Gordon was interested in everything. Kathy read aloud to him by the hour. Poetry, mostly—and he didn't seem to mind if she stumbled over strange words. She let him teach her to play chess with the board on his bedside table. He wanted to know all the hospital gossip, and charmed everybody from the cleaning woman to Miss Vale, the head nurse on the day shift.

Kathy was content to see him getting better steadily. She was grateful for his tact in treating her with the same impersonal friendliness that he showed to others in the hospital.

Now that he was convalescing so nicely, his mother came to see him only once a day—and briefly. She seemed very busy and bustled in and out. However, as the weeks went by, Kathy seldom found Gordon without company.

One day, when he had been in the hospital about three weeks, she ran by between class and three o'clock duty to bring him a bunch of freesias. She heard Gordon's voice, then a feminine voice, half-familiar but too muffled to recognize. As she debated whether to knock or go away, Gordon called out, "Kathy? You're just the person we need."

She came in and saw Evelyn, the tray girl, by the bureau. The girl's eyes were red and she was wadding one of Gordon's handkerchiefs in her hand. What was a tray girl doing there in the middle of the afternoon? What business did she have pouring out her troubles to a heart patient who needed peace and quiet? Kathy's professional and mother-hen instincts prompted her to shoo the girl away. The look on Gordon's face stopped her.

"Do you mind, Evelyn, if I ask you to begin at the beginning and tell Miss Martin the whole story?"

"You tell her. I told you you could, but she won't believe it. Nobody will." Evelyn broke down and sobbed.

"Hadn't I better take her outside? This can't be good for you, Gordon." Kathy was distressed.

"Oh, but it is," Gordon answered unexpectedly. "Makes me a full-fledged member of the Do-It-Yourself Agency. It's good for Miss—for Evelyn, too. She's been holding back long enough."

"Mike said I ought to have confessed and got it over with. But I knew I'd lose my job, and it's fun working here where he is." Evelyn stopped to blow her nose.

"Her fiance, Mike Padrone, is the grounds man," Gordon explained. "Seems I left my watch on the lunch tray. Careless of me! She very kindly brought it back fifteen or twenty minutes ago. She fished it out of her pocket from among various objects—one of which I couldn't identify by sound. Evelyn afterward told me it was a doughnut."

"It was from my lunch, Miss Martin. Mike gets awfully hungry digging and puttering in those flower beds. I wouldn't steal anything—not even a doughnut, much less that locket!"

"Gordon! You've found Mrs. Thomas' locket!" Kathy forgot nursing ethics and gave him a hug.

"Evelyn found it—in the same way and same place that she found my watch."

"Lots of things go out on the trays, Miss Martin. You'd be surprised. We take 'em back to the owner when the noon rush is over."

"I wondered how Evelyn knew the watch belonged to me," Gordon broke in. "Thought perhaps because the numbers on the dial are raised. I'm afraid I embarrassed her by being so frank about my disability. She assured me she hadn't thought of such a thing and pointed out my name card from the tray, tied to the wrist band. She'd learned that lesson, she said, if nothing else in her lifetime. Obviously, I wondered at her vehemence."

"Obviously, Sherlock, my boy." Kathy saw that Gordon was proud of picking up that clue so neatly. If the tray girl had forgotten to attach Mrs. Thomas' name to the locket, she might very well have been at a loss as to the owner. But why hadn't she turned it into Lost and Found? What a lot of suffering would have been saved!

"You could have turned the locket in at the office, Evelyn, or to the head nurse."

"I meant to, honest I did. But when it came time to go home, it wasn't there! I pulled everything out and looked all over. But I suppose I didn't worry about it the way I ought to have. I thought it would turn up by morning."

"But a valuable thing like that!" Kathy said.

Gordon leaned forward. "The girl didn't know until after it was lost that it was anything more than a trinket, Kathy. I can see, can't you, that if there was a big hullaballoo raised about the theft—"

"I knew nobody would believe me. You don't now, Miss Martin. Go on and report me. I'm glad he found out. Even if I lose my job—even if I go to jail."

Kathy thought hard. Evelyn's confession certainly proved Helene Stein's innocence, and Cranshaw's—though nobody had really seemed to take Mrs. Thomas seriously when she accused Mary. Unless the locket could be produced and returned to the owner, nothing would be gained by raising questions of Evelyn's guilt or innocence in anybody's mind.

"I do believe you," Kathy said slowly. "And I'm not going to make a report to the office. Not yet, anyhow. We'll just keep looking for the locket. It's no use stirring up any more trouble."

"You're not going to say anything?" Evelyn drew a deep breath that ended in a sigh.

"We'll have to tell a few people. Miss Johnson—when I go upstairs. She'll tell Mrs. Stein. And then my friends who've been helping solve the mystery must be told. They'll find the locket if anyone can. We don't need to tell anyone else."

"You forgot Mike," Gordon chuckled when the girl had left the room. "Unless I miss my guess, he'll know before you can say 'doughnut.' "

Kathy picked up Gordon's watch and strapped it on his wrist. "Golly! I'm five minutes late for duty!"

She took the back stairs, deciding that was quicker than the elevator, and so missed seeing Gordon's mother and Kelley deep in conversation in the little alcove by the elevators.

Kelley had been going off duty when Mrs. McKinlay stopped her to ask a question. "Mrs. McKinlay ought to know that nurses can't give out any information. That— and a few other little things—is what doctors are for," Kelley thought. Besides, she just didn't like Mrs. Mc-Kinlay very much. She stopped with reluctance.

"I just wondered if you had any idea when my son will be dismissed from the hospital?" Mrs. McKinlay was saying.

"None at all," Kelley answered.

The woman ignored the crisp tone and went on to explain. "I have decided to take Gordon to London. My husband is there and has talked to a very good doctor— not that Ash isn't good or that anyone can do much in these cases. Our boy has had this condition in his heart from birth. But a change of environment is often good, and my husband can make his headquarters one place as well as another."

Kelley was only half-listening. Her feet hurt and she was hungry. She was about to make some excuse to get away when the significance of Mrs. McKinlay's statement struck her. She decided to ask a question herself.

"Does Kathy know of your decision, Mrs. McKinlay? She's my roommate and—" Mrs. McKinlay, obviously, didn't think Kathy was good enough for her son.

"Kathy is partly the reason for the decision, Miss Jones. I blame myself for throwing her and Gordon together so much. Gordon has such a zest for living and his hold on life has always been precarious. I've tried to surround him with young people, as I have with books and music. I hadn't considered that it might mean heartache to someone—even to Gordon himself."

"Is Gordon willing to go along with your plans?" Kelley asked bluntly. "He and Kathy seem very much wrapped up in one another."

Mrs. McKinlay put her hand on Kelley's arm. "It was his idea," she confessed. "He wants to go far away because he's beginning to care too much for Kathy. But I thought—for Kathy's sake—I'd be the one to tell her. What do you think?"

Kelley had tears in her eyes. "I'd been thinking all the time you were the 'Mom' type, wanting to keep your wonderful son—and he *is* wonderful—to yourself. I couldn't have been more mistaken. Yes, I'd tell Kathy, if I were you. I think it will be easier for both of them. But not right away. I imagine Dr. Ash will want to keep his patient in the hospital until about the first of April, especially if he has a long trip ahead of him."

•   •   •

It was the first week of April. Kathy was on duty in the Recovery Room when Gordon was dismissed from the hospital. She had told him good-by the night before. The parting had been tearful on her side, reserved and carefully prepared on his.

The Recovery Room was long and bare. The patients, brought here from the operating table to be watched from one to five hours, had no need of beautiful surroundings. They rarely opened their eyes to the world until they were in their rooms. Recovery Room nursing required skill and could be very exacting. At the moment, however, Kathy had only one patient and he was sleeping quietly. Another operation was in progress. Her duties would be heavier soon.

Now she had time to stand at the window overlooking the path leading to the street—"her" path, flanked by the cafeteria on one side and the long flower bed on the other.

She saw Mrs. McKinlay cross the street to the parking lot and get in her car. A few moments later the car pulled to the curb at the end of the path.

It would have been nice to open the window and lean out to watch Gordon wheeled the whole length of the path. But in the Recovery Room, the window is never opened. Kathy pressed her head against it.

After a few minutes' wait she saw Tillie pushing the wheel chair briskly along. Sandy kept pace close to the wheel. Gordon didn't like wheel chairs, but it was the rule of the hospital that patients must be transported to their cars.

Halfway down the path, Kathy saw him cock his head to one side as if listening to some unusual noise. At a gesture from him, Tillie slowed down, then after a moment pushed the chair along the path to the curb.

Gordon was out of the chair before anyone could help him. He didn't move like a sick man. His mouth opened the car door and Kathy caught sight of a neat pile of suitcases. They intended going directly to the airport.

Mrs. McKinlay caught sight of Kathy at the third-floor window and waved. She touched Gordon on the arm. He looked up almost as if he could see her. Then he was gone.

CHAPTER XV

Kathy Writes a Letter

"If there's one place less interesting than Central Supply on day shift, it's Central Supply from eleven at night to seven in the morning," Kelley grumbled. She had been on "graveyard" shift ever since the day Gordon McKinlay had left the hospital and had scarcely seen Kathy. They met by chance at the elevator.

"Recovery Room duty hasn't been wildly exciting," Kathy said. "But for once I don't mind a dull assignment."

Kelley looked at the circles under her roommate's eyes and the drooping line of her mouth, and didn't like what she saw. She muttered something about the educational benefits derived from eight hours a day of moping.

"It's not moping," Kathy insisted. "It's a matter of thinking things through."

"You had a letter from Gordon?" Kelley had seen the onionskin envelope postmarked London.

Kathy flushed. She was glad that the elevator came at this moment. She didn't want to discuss Gordon with Kelley, and indeed had avoided conversation, as much as she could, with anyone. For a week she had watched the mail, hoping for a letter, yet afraid to expect one. Yesterday it had come, postmarked London. The single sheet of onionskin paper, already crumpled and dog-eared from being read so often, was in her pocket. She had shown it to no one and did not intend to.

Kathy nodded to a group of nurses in the hall and went immediately to put on her covering apron and sur-gical cap. She crossed the hall to the Recovery Room without stopping for the usual morning briefing. It was Tuesday morning, and that meant tonsils.

She busied herself setting out trays and instruments, checking the oxygen tank for use in case of emergency. Actually, there wasn't much to do, but she made each task last as long as possible. If you were busy, you didn't have to think.

Miss Johnson wheeled in the first patient—the small, limp figure of a boy about Johnny's age.

"Tonsillectomy," Miss Johnson said as she bent down to turn the child's head a little more to one side. "There are five more scheduled for this morning. The school-vacation rush. Let me know if you need help."

Postoperative care for the removal of tonsils was tricky. You had to guard against hemorrhage. And the opera-tion required very little anesthetic. The patients regained consciousness quickly. A few were frightened and need-ed comforting. But the little boy who looked like Johnny felt so well that he was bouncy. He demanded the pep-permint ice cream that he had been promised by his mother, and had to be distracted by a long nonsense story of an elephant who was a taster in a peppermint ice-cream factory.

It was noon before the last child was trundled off to the Pedie Ward. It was Kathy herself who took the child down. She felt rewarded for her morning's valiant efforts when the small girl looked up from the guerney and said, "Thank you very much. I've had a nice time."

There was only one patient in Recovery when she returned from lunch. The R.N. in charge handed over the chart with evident relief.

"Exploratory operation. Stomach ulcers. Doctor Beck's patient. Take pulse and blood pressure every ten minutes," she said. "Doctor Beck says he doesn't anticipate trouble. Just the usual extra precautions because of the age of the patient."

Kathy looked at the sleeping figure, then at the chart. *Aaron Gutman—age 80 years.*

"Thanks for taking over," she said, as the nurse hurried away. "Hope you're not perishing of hunger." She picked up the instrument for taking blood pressure, wound the band on a limp, bony arm, checked the two pressures. Then she counted the pulse and recorded everything on the chart. She settled down in a chair by the window with nothing to do for the next ten minutes.

Almost without thinking she pulled Gordon's letter from her pocket and spread it on the table to read for what seemed the hundredth time.

Dear Kathy,

We've had a pleasant and uneventful trip. So far, the only excitement was at the Chicago airport, where Sandy was nearly blown across the field and I felt somewhat like the tail of a kite. Sandy seems not to object to flying, however, provided it is done by the plane and not by her.

Was it only yesterday that we said good-by? The speed of jet transportation does strange things. It is not a matter of shrinking distance at all, in spite of the inevitable "small world" comments. Rather, I'd say that time stretches out like weak elastic. Speed serves only to make greater the distance between our yesterdays and our tomorrows. Or perhaps the strangeness comes from the feeling that "Thus far the miles are measured from my friend."

We'll land in England in a couple of hours. The present plan is to explore for a few weeks (including, of course, a pilgrimage to Canterbury), and then I'll be at the University of London working out some language experiments. Sandy's nose is already quivering at the promise of new sounds and smells, and I must confess to sharing her excitement.

Herewith a very lumpy couplet composed on the way to the airport yesterday morning:

Remember me, my Kathy, after your fashion
As you come to know love's passion from compassion.

Yours,

GORDON

P.S. Has it occurred to the Do-It-Yourself Detective Agency that their case began in September (what did you tell me was planted in the hospital garden then?) and that, spring being what it is, lost-and-found operations might profitably be carried on out-of-doors?

Of two things she was sure. First, that the letter said good-by. Good-by, period—unless perhaps you read between the lines. (Did "Yours" at the end mean *hers*—or was it short for "*Yours truly,*" like a business letter?) Second, it was clear that Gordon thought she pitied him, sympathized with him—and that she did not know love from sympathy! And he was so wrong!

With an eye on the time, she interrupted her thoughts at regular intervals to check blood pressure and pulse. The patient was resting quietly.

The letter didn't require an answer, she admitted to herself. But it was going to get one anyway, and in poetry. You could say things with a poem that you couldn't say any other way.

Three o'clock came at last. Dr. Beck came in and helped Kathy trundle the old man to his room in the new wing. An R.N. came on for the evening shift in Recovery, and Kathy was free to explore the stacks at the college library for just the right poem to convince Gordon of her true feelings.

"A sonnet is what I want," she said to herself as she trudged across the green she had so often walked with Gordon. Sonnets were his favorite form of verse.

Until she had started reading aloud to him, she hadn't known exactly what a sonnet was, except that it had fourteen lines and that you had to memorize one by Shakespeare in high-school English class.

"Shall I compare thee to a summer's day"—that had

been Kathy's assignment. The other thirteen lines were erased from her mind until Gordon recited the poem one day and made it sound fresh and new. Shakespeare had written a hundred and fifty-three other sonnets. Surely, one of them would help her show Gordon her true feelings.

But hours of search through Shakespeare and Milton and half a dozen anthologies failed to uncover just the right poem. There was one by John Milton that almost made her cry. Milton was blind—like Gordon: a blind poet.

Her face was veiled, yet to my fancied sight
Love, sweetness, goodness in her person shined
So clear as in no face with more delight.
But O, as to embrace me she inclined,
I waked, she fled, and day brought back my night.

"'And day brought back my night.'" She whispered the line. "But it was Gordon who fled, not I. And all I want is the opportunity to bring day into his night—for the rest of his life."

"Be my eyes," Gordon had said that time under the redwood trees. Yet through his sightless eyes he had shown her new kinds of beauty. And he had shown her courage, too.

She'd have to make up a sonnet herself. She tore a piece of paper out of her notebook, headed it carefully "To Gordon, Upon Parting."

Be my eyes—those were the words you said
While we walked the wooded path—

No. It wasn't right to begin by reminding him of his blindness.

What words will show how dear you are to me?
How can I prove what you will not believe?
Shall I confess the way my heart does grieve
Now that you've gone across the wayward sea?

"But I can't take up fourteen lines asking questions," Kathy said aloud. Ten lines left, to explain that he was gallant and gay and brave—that all she asked was to be beside him when he needed her. She closed her eyes, remembering the days that she had walked alone, trying to feel what it would be like never to see the springtime, yet to know it through the other senses.

Two tears splashed down on the paper. She stared at it. *Believe, grieve, leave* . . . for the life of her, she couldn't think of another rhyming word. What was wrong? Suddenly she tore the scrap of paper into bits and flung the pieces in the waste basket. She picked up the books and almost ran from the library.

Compassion, passion—was it true that she didn't know the difference? She made her way across campus in the dusk, driven by the turmoil of confused thought.

"Miss Martin—your posture!"

Miss Wilson's sharp voice brought Kathy up short. The stiff little figure was almost hidden behind a bag of groceries.

"If you're going my way, perhaps you'd carry this bag into the house for me. It's more your size than mine."

Kathy didn't want to say yes, but she couldn't say no. Silently she took the groceries and walked beside the school director to the tiny cottage.

"Just set them in the kitchen," Miss Wilson said crisply. "And turn the gas on under the kettle. We'll have some tea. I'm pleased that we met, Miss Martin. I've been planning to suggest a conference."

"Now, what have I done?" Kathy thought to herself. Had Miss Johnson told how they'd suspected Mrs. Stein? Or had Miss Vale reported that she'd overstayed her coffee break the other day, tearing a cupboard to pieces in a fruitless search for the locket?

Miss Wilson busied herself setting out cups and cookies for tea. She made no effort to carry on a conversation until they were seated in the living room with the tea tray between them. Then she spoke more gently than usual.

"One of the difficult things for a student nurse to learn," she said, "is to refrain from becoming emotionally involved with patients. Especially if the patient is young and attractive."

"How did you know?" Kathy blurted out the words before she could stop herself.

Miss Wilson seemed not to notice the interruption. "Yet it is not quite the case, is it, that we want to feel *nothing* toward our patients?"

"I wasn't on duty in Med-Surg when Gordon McKinlay had the heart attack." Kathy was close to tears. "He—he was my friend."

Miss Wilson set a box of Kleenex beside Kathy without seeming to notice the choked-up voice and the tears.

"Sometimes the hardest part for a young nurse is to recognize her own emotion for what it is. She may imagine that she is in love."

Kathy suddenly pulled the crumpled letter out of her pocket and handed it to Miss Wilson. While the older woman read, she took advantage of the pause to wipe her eyes.

"Hmph!" Miss Wilson spoke disapprovingly. "Entirely without meter. A very poor couplet indeed. But while the young man hasn't produced a line of poetry, he has shown a maturity of understanding beyond my expectation. Would you say that he is correct in his judgment?"

After a few minutes, Kathy looked up. "I expect it's my pride that's hurt, partly," she said half to herself. "I thought it would be wonderful to spend my life taking care of somebody who needed me—somebody who was gallant and brave. . . . And I thought he *did* need me."

"In our profession there's no lack of opportunities for service, my child." Miss Wilson permitted herself the ghost of a smile. "But service is not the whole of living."

She held out Gordon's letter. "Rather a cryptic post-script, isn't it?"

Kathy glanced at the bottom of the page and blushed. "I'm afraid I didn't pay much attention to the post-script, Miss Wilson."

To cover her confusion, she launched into the story of Mrs. Stein and the lost locket, and somehow she got onto Linda and the pancakes. Anything to keep from talking about Gordon! It would take her a little time to face up to the truth.

"Does Mrs. Stein want to return to nursing?"

"Oh, yes. Linda—she's on duty in the surgical ward where Mrs. Stein is—she says they talk about it all the time. But I don't see how she can afford it."

"Good nurses are in demand," Miss Wilson said thoughtfully. "I think we can arrange a scholarship from the Big Sister Fund. In fact, I'm sure of it."

"Are you really, Miss Wilson?" Kathy's eyes glowed.

"So sure that I think you and Miss Garfield could tell her, if you like. To have something to look forward to will be good therapy."

Kathy did not see the look on Miss Wilson's face as she watched the tall, straight figure in white swinging down the street. Having something to look forward to was good therapy for a student nurse, too!

At home, Kathy moved a palette and brushes off the desk (Kelley had taken up oil painting again) and fished in the drawer for stationery. She unfolded Gordon's letter and read the postscript carefully for the first time.

Has it occurred to the Do-It-Yourself Detective Agency that their case began in September (What did you tell me was planted in the hospital garden then?) and that, spring being what it is, lost-and-found operations might profitably be carried on out-of-doors?

September . . . and that spring being what it is, lost-and-found operations might be carried on out-of-doors? What on earth was Gordon talking about? It would be quite in order to write and ask him what he meant—in just the tone in which he'd written to her.

"*Dear Gordon,*" she wrote. "I'm writing this after duty in the Recovery Room, where they take all the patients after operations. I'm on PM shift (3-11) and business ь slow, so I've had lots of time to think—"

Too much time, Kathy said to herself, and went on quickly.

"—about the mystery of the locket and about the postscript to your letter. But I still don't understand what you meant about looking for the locket in the great outdoors. Tray girls wear out their shoes traveling the high road between the kitchen and the upstairs corridors. The pocket Evelyn lost the thing out of (excuse the grammar) was an apron pocket, and aprons only go outside in a laundry bag—so how could the locket have gotten outdoors?

"By now I suppose you have made your pilgrimage to Canterbury and are ready to start your new studies. But I hope you can find the time, Mr. Sherlock Holmes, to give us a clue. We all miss you. Give Sandy a pat for me."

She hesitated a moment, then firmly signed her name and slipped the letter into an envelope, just as Linda entered the room.

"I've decided!" Linda announced with her usual breathless enthusiasm.

Kathy laughed. "Decided what? To marry Jim Telford and support him through medical school in the style to which he isn't accustomed?"

Linda blushed. "We're not even engaged, Martin! Wearing a fraternity pin isn't an engagement. I've decided on my Senior Service. I'm going to ask for med-surg. You really see more of the patients on Second West than anywhere else. Get to know people better, don't you think so?"

Know people? I don't even know myself. Kathy bent over the sealed envelope and addressed it carefully.

"I'd thought of med-surg, too," she said, slowly. "But I think I'll ask for Nursery. I love working with the newborn babies."

"So do I!" Linda wrinkled her brow. "Diapering and bathing and feeding. And that lovely moment when you carry them to their mothers! Kathy, I thought I *had* made a hard, firm decision—and now you've unsettled me again!"

Never again would she think of the woman as aloof and austere!

Kathy was charting her third entry when a sound brought her to her feet. Was the patient already showing signs of restlessness? No. There was something wrong. She took a step, then stopped to listen an instant more.

Hard, short breaths. There was some difficulty with circulation. Kathy counted the pulse. Fast and irregular —not slow, as it would be in postoperative shock or anesthesia reaction. Color—bad. Even as she counted the pulse, the patient's face turned from pale to a reddish flush. Then came the faint beginnings of the blue of cyanosis.

Over and over during Nursing Arts classes, the students were required to act out emergency situations. Kathy felt now as if she were hearing Mrs. Seaforth rap out vital symptoms. As if she were practicing, Kathy's hands responded, without thought, without waste motion.

She flashed the emergency light to signal for assistance, and crossed the room in long strides to get the oxygen tank ready.

Place the cup over the patient's nostrils. Adjust valves. Keep the oxygen going.

Miss Johnson and the surgeon pushed open the door. For minutes the three worked as a team. Color returned to Mrs. Stein's face. Her pulse steadied.

For an instant the patient came to. "Elena!"

"The child is well, Helene." Miss Johnson's hands rested lightly but firmly on the sheet.

"I thought we were together," Mrs. Stein murmured thickly. She opened her eyes.

"You will be soon," Kathy whispered.

The woman's eyes closed, and she dozed peacefully.

The surgeon put away his stethoscope. "One of these days we'll whip this business of operative reactions," he said. "I think I can get coffee now. Call me in the cafeteria if you need me, Miss Martin. And let me know when Mrs. Stein is ready to go to her room. About a half hour, I'd say."

It was not until she was alone with the patient that Kathy realized her knees were knocking together. It would have been awful if anything had happened—just when Mrs. Stein had so much to live for!

Just before three o'clock, Kathy pushed the guerney down the corridor. Linda met her at the Nurse's Station on Third East.

"Everything okay?"

Kathy nodded. "Everything," she said.

year just for the Senior class. "If boy friends were invited," Kathy said to herself ruefully, "Steve wouldn't be among those present."

She hadn't seen him at all since she broke the Yosemite date to go to Gordon's graduation. That had been last February, and now it was May. After she had refused to go to San Francisco when he got his promotion, Steve had simply bowed himself out of the picture. Yet, here she was wondering what he'd say about a dress he'd probably never see.

She wasn't the first to get home. Gail was ahead of her, standing on tiptoe in the hall solemnly marking a line through the date on the calendar at the top of the bulletin board.

"May fifteenth," she said. "Only a hundred days left till the wedding!"

"You don't need tonight's crystal ball to see the future, do you? How's the cooking?"

Gail had surprised them all by choosing the diet kitchen for her Senior Service.

"Journalists have to eat," she explained. "I'll be working wherever Matt gets a job, and dietitians are always in demand."

The banquet was at a downtown hotel. Yo's sister had been in charge of the decorations. She had hung lovely, iridescent balloons from the ceiling. They looked like crystal when the candlelight reflected from them. A bank of Miss Merriweather's lilacs and twenty-nine girls in their best evening dresses made even the inevitable chicken and peas and mashed potatoes seem glamorous. The ice cream was topped with perky spun-sugar nurses' caps. With the coffee, the singing began—songs from all their shows since Probie days.

> *We're just Probies, Baby Probies,*
> *We have come here straight from Mars.*

> *We're the Juniors,*
> *We're the Juniors,*
> *And we never, never boast.*
> *We'll just show you,*
> *When we know you,*
> *That the Juniors are the most!*

"How come they're all to the tune of *Clementine?*" whispered Mary Cranshaw.

Kathy laughed. "They have to be. That's the only tune I can carry!"

While they were singing, Mary slipped from the room to return in gypsy costume. She was dragging an IV standard from which was suspended, neither a jar of blood plasma nor the all-too-familiar glucose and water, but a crystal ball for telling what the future held for each member of the Senior Class.

The years of training were so nearly over that every one of the Seniors had "where to, what next?" in the front of her thoughts. They looked forward to the prophecies with almost superstitious awe.

For Ann Cooper, the class president, the gypsy promised two more years of study at college:

> *"She'll study for five years instead of three*
> *To earn the coveted B.S. degree.*
> *B.S. and R.N. What a brain!*
> *As head nurse she'll surely reign."*

Jenny, the gypsy predicted, would become The World's Best Visiting Nurse, while Linda would "go through life a doctor's wife."

Yo, the scientist, would "climb the ladder of fame with an M.D. after her name."

To Kelley, her Big Sister, Mary said with a mischievous grin:

> *"Don't look now, but your heart is showin'.*
> *Deny, if you can, that it belongs to Bowen."*

Kathy's prophecy was the last of the fifteen.

> *"In nurse's cap, she'll stand up tall,*
> *The reigning queen of the Fireman's Ball."*

Tears came to Kathy's eyes as the girls applauded. She'd probably never see Steve again, much less go to a dance with him.

CHAPTER XVII

Where To? What Next?

As if to prove Mary's fortune-telling totally without foundation, Kelley began playing the game *Where to? What next?* with maps. One day she would announce that she was thinking of taking a job in the Fiji Islands. A few days later the map of Brazil was pinned to the window curtain, and she was preparing to learn Portuguese. For three days she dieted, because if she could lose the five pounds she had put on this year she could become an airline stewardess on a Red Cross hospital plane.

Kathy didn't take her roommate's trips around the globe seriously until the Saturday afternoon when she came back from a ride with Linda and Jim up Mount Hamilton. Kelley had refused to go along on the ground that she hadn't even cut the pages of the book on obstetrical nursing. However, the book lay on the corner of the desk as fresh and untouched as a new-minted coin. The floor, the beds, the one easy chair were covered with maps, pamphlets and open copies of an official-looking magazine—*Federal Native Service, Headquarters, Sitka, Alaska.*

"You get there by a plane that lands in the fjord outside some other town and then you take a ferry. The ferryman is an Eskimo with a college education. He takes a charming picture—high cheek bones and a dimple in his chin and eyes that say 'Come on, World!' But I suppose his charms are irrelevant, because the ferry ride lasts only five minutes."

"Where did all this stuff about Alaska come from?" Kathy looked around the room, estimating how many wastebaskets the maps and pamphlets would fill when her roommate decided she'd rather investigate Australia.

Kelley blushed. "Doctor Bowen sent for it. He spent his residency at the hospital there. It's a Federal institution, mostly for the natives. Big. Spreads over three islands. Ought to improve my swimming."

Kathy studied the maps. "How far away is Alaska, anyway?"

"Only a thousand miles if I get assigned to Sitka—two thousand if they send me up to the Arctic Circle. I'm filling out my application now. Bowen brought the whole batch by right after lunch. He says they need nurses."

"Jonesy! Is this for real?"

"They might not take me," Kelley answered. "They ask everything on this application except what I eat for breakfast. And Bowen is writing a letter saying that though I've had no experience— Hey! Speaking of letters, you've got two. Under that map, near the North Pole."

Kathy fished for her mail. One from her mother, the other air-mailed from London.

Kathy tore open the thin onionskin envelope, read the typed letter through and sat staring off in space, the single sheet of paper folded under both hands.

Kelley raised her head questioningly. They always shared their letters with each other. "From Gordon?" she asked with a casualness that was plainly assumed.

Kathy shook her head. "From his mother. Gordon's had another attack. He's under an oxygen tent."

She held out the letter and Kelley crossed the room to read it.

"It says here he's doing well and has good care."

"Yes," Kathy said. "He'll probably get over this attack. And then he'll have another. And another. Not many more, though. The human system can't take it forever." She talked half to herself.

"Maybe knowing he might die any time was what gave his life such zest." Kelley felt her way. She couldn't tell what Kathy was thinking.

"That and his blindness. Every day was new," Kathy answered slowly. "Simple experiences, the sound of the brook in Big Basin, children playing around a park bench. Everything had a fresh meaning for him."

Kelley was still scanning Mrs. McKinlay's brief note. "What's this about not being able to answer questions?"

"The thing we didn't understand—about looking for the locket outside the hospital," Kathy said. "Gordon is a wonderful person, Kelley, but I feel sad about him the way you do about a patient, not like—like—"

"Somebody you imagined yourself in love with?" Kelley finished the sentence brusquely. "Look," she said, "why don't you come with me to Alaska? The contracts run for a year and we'll get all kinds of nursing experience."

"I've half a mind to," Kathy said. "I'd have to see what the family thinks and—"

She left the words in mid-air, and Kelley knew she was wondering about Steve.

"I can ask for an application for you when I forward mine to Washington," Kelley said. "You don't have to make it out if you change your mind."

CHAPTER XVIII

The Patient on Third East

Kathy stopped at the foot of the Senior Residence steps and sniffed the June morning.

"What do I smell? It's too late for winter fog, too early for cannery smog. But there's something funny in the air."

Jenny had followed her out of the house. They were both bound for the AM shift.

"You don't listen to the radio, don't read the newspapers. Just get up and rush over to the Nursery to see what new infants have been born during the night."

"Okay, Miss Well-informed Ramirez, what's going on?" Kathy persisted.

"Big Basin is on fire."

Kathy slowed her pace. "Not the redwoods!" A sharp image of those great, growing columns and green boughs meeting overhead was etched on her mind. And, since she had seen the Big Basin Forest only once, the picture was peopled, indistinctly, with the figures of herself and Gordon. But almost instantly Big Basin itself was blotted out by the thought of what forest fires meant. There'd been times when, worried about Steve, she'd hung on the phone in Appleton trying to get news of forest fires in the neighborhood.

They were frightening, and if you knew someone out there struggling against smoke and crashing branches and the oncoming flames, you didn't forget it. Steve had been out three days last summer fighting a blaze in the hills. But late August and September usually was the season to worry about forest fires—not June. She studied the sky to the south. There was a definite, telltale, blue haze.

"Big Basin is twenty-five miles away," she said. "The fire must be serious for us to get a whiff of it this far away."

Jenny nodded. "Last night's paper was full of it. They're redeploying fire departments for fifty miles around. San Tomás is sending a unit down."

At the door of the hospital they went separate ways. Kathy fumbled in her pocket for a dime to buy a newspaper before she went up to the maternity wing to report for duty. Headlines and pictures of the fire covered half the front page. But it was the fine print that took Kathy's eye. There was a list of towns that had sent units of fire fighters to Big Basin, from up and down the coast, from Monterey, twenty-five miles south of Appleton, to Half Moon Bay, north of San Tomás. Steve was probably at Big Basin now—or on his way.

She'd thought she was going to see Steve last weekend. Gail and Matt had driven down the coast below Appleton. They had offered to drop Kathy off at home for a few hours and pick her up on the way back, and she had gone with more eagerness than she liked to admit.

It was lovely to be home, and she'd had the chance to show her family the application for the Alaska job and see what they thought about it. But Steve wasn't in town. He'd gone to Denver for some kind of fire-fighters' conference. Nick had volunteered the information almost as soon as she stepped in the house. As if she'd come to see Steve instead of them!

Well, she had. After the Senior banquet she had written a letter, but she hadn't mailed it. You couldn't say, *Do you remember me? I'm the girl you had a date with.* And Steve hadn't made it any easier by his own silence.

Going up in the elevator, she studied the pictures of the fire. One of the firemen handling an ax looked as big as Steve, but the photograph was blurred by the smoke. You couldn't make out any of the faces.

When Kathy got to the Nursery, it was time for team conference. The team leader was an R.N. who had been in charge of the Nursery for years. Other nurses and students and aides came and went. Miss Ellery stayed on. She wouldn't accept any other job. The newborns were her whole life.

Every day the tiny inhabitants of the bassinets changed. When "old-timers," four days or a week old, went home, new arrivals took their places. The "preemies" in the incubators stayed longer, sometimes as much as a month. To Miss Ellery, and to all the students who came under her training, there were no "cases" in the Nursery—just babies to be cared for and loved and properly admired.

There were nine infants in cribs and one little four-pounder in an incubator. Before the brief conference was over, an eleventh was brought in by the nurse from OB. The tiny girl had been foot-printed for identification. Her fat little ankle was banded with a pink bracelet, and she was dressed and swaddled in a blanket. To Kathy fell the privilege of taking the newborn from the OB nurse and laying her in her crib.

It was not until noon that Kathy heard anything more about the forest fire. She bought another paper and was reading it while she ate her lunch. Just then, Yo came into the cafeteria—grinning broadly, her black eyes sparkling with excitement.

"The hospital is sending a first-aid unit down to Big Basin. And I'm elected! Mostly R.N.'s, and lab technicians to give plasma—and me."

"That's super!" Kathy felt a twinge of envy, but, of course, Yo was the best in their class at giving plasma transfusions. And that was what the serious burn cases would require.

"You might see Steve down at Big Basin," Kathy said very casually. "If you do see him, would you give him my love."

Yo was not deceived by the casual manner. "If I hear anything, Kathy, do you want me to call you?"

Kathy blushed. It was no use pretending with Yo or with Kelley. Or with Gail or Linda or Jenny. "Would you? Be sure to leave a message if I'm not home."

Next morning, when the baths were just about over and the hungriest of the newborns were letting out lusty cries so that the Nursery sounded like a cat fight or a jazz combo tuning up, Miss Ellery came in.

"A telephone call, Martin. Somebody in Third East from your home town would like to see you. I'll carry on here, till you get back. It's Room 370. Kelvick or Kovak was the name, I think."

When Kathy entered the room, Steve was sitting up in a chair. He had a plaster cast on his left arm.

"Oh, Steve!" Kathy burst into tears.

Steve patted her shoulder awkwardly with his good hand. "It's nothing to make a fuss about. Just a broken wrist."

"Is it very painful? Did they give you plenty of pain-killer?"

"No and yes, in the order named. I'm all right. Guess I have to be a patient to get proper attention from you." The words were said lightly, but Steve was only half-joking.

Kathy glanced across the room at the other bed. The stranger was politely studying the ceiling. "But you're *not* my patient!" she told Steve in a muffled voice.

"I'm all right, Kathy. I'm practically dismissed. They just kept me overnight because I had a little smoke inside me. That thing at Big Basin is bad. Worst in the Valley in years."

"What time did they bring you in?" She could read about Big Basin in the newspapers.

"About eleven last night, I'd guess. Jenny Ramirez held my hand till the anesthetist put me under. The arm hurt. Until it was set, that is."

"Jenny didn't tell me," Kathy's lips trembled.

"I wouldn't let her. Needed a night's sleep and a shave before I saw my girl. It's been—a long time."

"Steve, I've missed you so. I *was* going to Alaska."

"Heard about it. Big Nick told me."

"I—I don't have to go—if you need me."

"Need you? For a broken bone? I'll be back in harness in a week, Kathy. Alaska and the Native Service sounds great. Especially with Kelley Jones along to look after you. I'd say go, while you have the chance."

That wasn't what she thought he'd say at all—not the way he was looking at her. Kathy stiffened. "You didn't miss me at all, Steve."

He took her hand in his and held it tight. "I missed you all right, and I don't want you to get *that* far away again. But Alaska's only a thousand miles."

"I've got to go back on duty, Steve."

"Sure you do. Hear you're taking Senior Service in the Nursery. You must be having a picnic with all those babies. Run along back to 'em. When I come up to have this cast taken off, maybe we can go dancing."

•   •   •

"Did you and Steve make it up?" Kelley asked bluntly, that evening.

Kathy chuckled. "I guess we did. Anyhow, we ended up scrapping—as usual. He'll be up next week to take me dancing when they take his cast off."

CHAPTER XIX

Hearts and Spades

"I'm never going to sit at this table next year," Linda said with a catch in her voice.

She was with Gail and Kathy at their favorite spot in the cafeteria, by the window that looked out on the flower beds. Of the third-floor gang, only Linda would be staying on as a nurse at San Tomás Hospital after graduation. "It just won't be the same without all of us together," she said mournfully.

"You'll have to keep us posted on the news." Gail smiled and pointed toward the window. "Season by season, with the flowers as your calendar. They're taking up the pansies and stock now, and putting in the zinnias—like last year. I wonder—"

"—whether they'll be in bloom for your wedding?" Linda chuckled. "I thought I recognized that dreamy look!"

Gail blushed. "Right. But I don't suppose zinnias would be proper for bridesmaids to carry, anyway."

The hundred days before Gail's wedding had shrunk to fifty. And now graduation was looming up like a mountain seen from a fast train. Final exams were over and only two weeks of Senior Service remained before the big day. Boxes of invitations covered the desks at senior residence, ready to be addressed and mailed.

"What a year it's been!" Linda exclaimed. "Isn't it wonderful that Mrs. Stein's started her course? Miss Johnson says she's like a different person. But I'll never live down the pancakes."

"Oh, you'll survive." There was a twinkle in Gail's eye. Linda didn't know that Jim's graduation present to her would be a griddle. Kathy and Gail had helped him pick it out—stainless steel, he had demanded, one that would last forever.

Gail winked at Kathy, but Kathy didn't respond. She wasn't listening. She had turned her chair around and was staring out of the window.

"Come over here a minute," she said.

Gail and Linda walked around the table and pressed their noses against the window.

It was a charming scene that they witnessed. Evelyn, the tray girl, had slipped out of the kitchen to the flower bed close by the wall, where Mike Padrone was busy taking out the overgrown stock and pansy plants. The two stood hand in hand for a moment, in earnest conference. Then Evelyn gave Mike a quick kiss and a slightly flattened doughnut which she fished out of her pocket. She stooped down to pick a pansy from one of the discarded plants, glanced hastily at an upstairs window, and darted out of sight in the direction of the diet kitchen.

"Hearts and spades?" Gail collected titles for plays the way small boys do baseball cards.

"Love in the blooms," Linda proposed. "Anyhow, it goes to prove that the way to a man's heart is through the stomach. I'll have to learn to make doughnuts by the time Jim finishes pre-med."

"You'd better stick to pancakes, my child," Gail said solemnly.

"Be quiet and close your eyes." The order, in a firm voice, came from Kathy. "Now," she went on, seriously, "get a line on that scene—or one like it—with other senses than sight. That's what Gordon McKinlay had to do. Of course, he knew about Evelyn's doughnuts. So did I. But I somehow never pictured her slipping out in the middle of a shift to feed her man."

"I would. Men get *awfully* hungry." Linda opened her blue eyes wide.

"That's just what Evelyn said. But don't you remember what Gordon wrote?"

Gail interrupted excitedly. "Anything could have fallen out of that girl's pocket, the way she was cavorting around. Okay, take this down, Dr. Watson: *Scene,* September the something—"

"I won't forget that date!" Kathy broke in. "The fourteenth. I thought I'd never want to be a team leader again!"

"All right," Gail went on. "The fourteenth of September: *Characters*: Mike Padrone, the grounds man. His girl. One crumbly doughnut. One wheelbarrow full of— What was he planting in September, Kathy?"

"Chrysanthemums. Those lovely purplish-crimson ones."

"Details of color may be left to the costume-and-props committee, Miss Martin. Where was I?" Gail frowned. "Wheelbarrow full of chrysanthemums. Mike. Evelyn. What else?"

Kathy giggled. "I once saw a performance of *Hamlet* with his father's ghost left out. It was pretty flat."

"What's that got to do with chrysanthemums?" Linda was bewildered by the conversation.

"Oh, good heavens!" Gail exclaimed. "You're right, Kathy. I was forgetting the corpse—I mean, the locket."

"Right," said Kathy. "The locket is probably right in front of our eyes. Only we can't see it, because it's in the ground!"

"You mean," said Linda, suddenly getting the idea— "you mean it might have dropped out of her pocket? And be buried in the flower bed?"

Kathy nodded. "I think we ought to tell Mike. He'll look for it, I'm sure."

"Not on your life!" Gail shook her head vigorously. "This job belongs to the Do-It-Yourself Detective Agency —including Miss Kelley Jones. You know how skeptical she's been about Evelyn's story of losing the thing."

"On the other hand, if we don't find it," Kathy said slowly, "she'll be sure that Evelyn stole it. She thinks I'm a sentimental softy for not reporting it to somebody. She has a point, too. If the story ever gets back to the powers that be, there'll be a lot of questions asked—like why we took it on ourselves to keep secrets from the administration. And so forth."

"All the more reason to look for it ourselves," said Gail triumphantly. "Agreed? We'll have to dig after dark. I'll get Matt and a lot of flashlights before tonight."

"Not tonight. Steve's coming up. We're supposed to go dancing, remember? I didn't think he was well enough the day he had his cast removed."

"Miss Martin!" Gail was wearing her severest expression. "Do you put dancing before digging? I fear I shall have to report you to your superiors in the Do-It-Yourself Detective—"

"You can't. She *is* her superiors," Linda said. "I mean, she's a charter member."

"Okay," Gail said. "Then she'll have to try herself. Court's in session. Martin versus Martin. Take the stand, Martin."

"It would be wonderful if Gordon had been right," Kathy was thinking out loud. "He's getting his strength back, but slowly, Mrs. McKinlay said in her last letter. How dumb he must think we are not to know enough to understand his clue! I guess I can make it tonight. Steve will understand—" She stopped short and bit her lip, suddenly remembering a day in the redwoods. "I mean, if we need Steve to help us, I'm sure he'll pitch in. Take a list, Gail. Spade, trowels, kitchen fork—"

"Colander to sift dirt," Linda added.

"Pancake turner, did you say?" Gail asked, and fled in a manner just barely suitable to the dignity of the profession.

•   •   •

When Kelley, Yo, and Jenny came out of the hospital after their PM shift, they moved quietly around to the flower bed near the kitchen window. Gail and Matt, Linda and Jim were guarding the strange-looking pile of equipment. A few minutes later, Steve's car pulled up to the curb.

"Why's Kathy all dressed up?" Linda whispered.

Kelley laughed. "She wasn't taking any chances. Said she wasn't going to say a word to Steve until they'd been on the dance floor an hour. Looks as if it agreed with both of them."

Half an hour later, the digging operations were in full swing. Kathy was sifting out a colander full of dirt when she heard Linda's gasp. She looked up to see Mrs. Seaforth striding down the hospital walk. Someone had telephoned from the hospital that the Seniors were up to some sort of high jinks.

"What *are* you doing?" she asked. "Burying your sins? Because if you're burying your stripes, you're about a week early."

Mrs. Seaforth was used to strange pregraduation ceremonies on the part of Senior nurses. The blue-and-white-striped uniforms worn on the last shift before graduation were, by tradition, disposed of in any way the nurses saw fit.

"We're not burying stripes or sins," Kathy explained a little nervously. "More like digging up our sins. Do you remember when we first began team leadership last year, and I made such a mess of it? I mean about Mrs. Thomas' locket. I never thought I'd be around for Senior Service."

Mrs. Seaforth frowned. "Nobody blamed *you* for that."

"I blame myself," Kathy said. "It certainly didn't put the hospital in a good light. And then it turned into such a tragedy about Mrs. Stein."

"Who is now in better shape than she's been for years." Mrs. Seaforth said firmly. "Don't be so hard on yourself, Kathy. Sometimes you have to show yourself the same tolerance you show others. That's not advice I'd give to many people, I admit."

There was a cry from the other end of the garden. It was Kelley who held up a muddy piece of jewelry.

The mud was scraped off and the locket passed from hand to hand.

"This calls for a celebration," said Jim.

"I know somebody who's going to celebrate," Kathy Thomas is going to be mighty pleased."

said. "I hadn't really thought of her, but Mrs. Marcelene

she said, "and I'll have to do the best I can with what I've learned."

Yo walked around the hospital, solemnly happy. Her brother, the lab technician, had offered to stake her to the first year at college in the long pull toward her medical career.

Linda's family—now as proud as they once were skeptical—were taking her on a trip abroad before she came back to do bedside nursing at San Tomás.

Their new "whites" were hanging in the closets, the last invitations mailed, the proofs of the programs approved. The last practice sing had been conducted by Gail. She had written the words of their graduation song to an old Spanish tune, and as they lined up for the procession she was as nervous as any Broadway producer before a first-night curtain.

The graduation exercises were to be held out-of-doors, on the rotunda of the main entrance of the hospital. Rows of seats for the audience had been set up under the trees.

"At least we don't have to worry about the weather," Kathy said. "It's a good thing we graduate in July instead of February."

"In February we wouldn't have to worry either," Kelley answered. "We'd know we'd have rain." The class was lined up according to height, so the two roommates were together—the last in line.

Yo, as the smallest, was at the front of the reception hall, where they were waiting for the moment when the heavy doors would open and they would make their first appearance in the white uniforms of graduate nurses. Yo stepped out of line and pushed a window curtain ever so slightly aside.

"The place is jammed!" she reported in an excited whisper. "Naturally it would be, with all our families. Linda, I see your mother—it *must* be, she looks so exactly like you. And Miss Merriweather, and Miss Covington. *She* looks a little flustered."

"As well she might," Kelley whispered to Kathy. "With the reception for us and our friends and relations in the old garden. I suppose Johnny will decorate the punch bowl as usual."

Johnny's disastrous entrance into the life of the San Tomás Nursing School in their Freshman year had never ceased to entertain her.

"Johnny?" Kathy shook her head. "He's grown three inches! I'm beginning to think he may not be the shrimp of the Martin family after all."

Yo dropped the curtain and stepped back into line. "The Juniors and Freshmen are walking in," she said with a sudden catch in her voice.

The Juniors, who would so soon be transformed into Seniors. And the Freshmen, who were no longer Probies!

"Get ready. The doors are going to open!" Gail said. "Kelley, don't forget to come in strong on your solo line!" She gave them the pitch for the song, raised her hand for a signal and brought it down with a clear, precise gesture. Then she stepped into place as the Senior Class marched out to receive their diplomas.

Kathy couldn't remember singing at all, but the song must have gone well, if you could judge by the applause. She couldn't remember a word of the speeches, either. She was glad that her family was sitting up front where she could see them. Johnny and Nick in Sunday suits were squirming a little on the narrow benches. But Big Nick sat with his arms folded, nodding agreement with whatever was being said. Kathy remembered how nervous he had been at her high-school graduation three years ago—how he'd lean forward with his huge farmer's hands gripping his knees when she stood up in her cap and gown to make the valedictory speech. Since then, her father had seen Nick get his diploma. "Now me again," Kathy said to herself, "with the kind of cap on my head I always wanted. Graduations are getting to be a habit with Papa. He's used to them. And I like Mama's new hat. Maybe because it looks just like the old ones." Her eyes kept moving over the audience. She didn't see Steve and he'd said he was coming. . .

It wasn't until her name was called and she stood up to cross the platform that she caught sight of the tall figure she was looking for. Steve was way off in left field leaning up against a tree.

"He could have sat down. The place isn't that crowded," she was thinking as the President of Trustees put her diploma in her hand. Two strides took her to Miss

Wilson, who smiled broadly as she reached up to fasten the school pin on Kathy's white uniform.

When all the diplomas had been presented and all fifteen graduate students had been "pinned" and had returned to their places, Mrs. Seaforth led the class in reciting the Florence Nightingale Pledge: *"I solemnly pledge myself before God and in the presence of this assembly. . . . With loyalty I will endeavor to aid the physician in his work and devote myself to the welfare of those committed to my care."*

It was all over, and time for the second verse of Gail's song. No—not quite! Dr. Smith was standing up to award the San Tomás Medical Staff Scholarship. "The Scholarship, to enable a student to carry on further studies, is this year awarded to Juanita Ramirez."

"Our Jenny!" Kathy gave Kelley such a pinch that her *ouch!* was barely drowned out by the applause of the audience.

"Ready," Gail whispered. This time she stood in front of the class to lead the song.

They had practiced the recessional the night before. Down the broad, stone steps in single file. Turn right at the foot of the stairs, form double line, then march past the row of blue-striped uniforms. "Don't look back. The Juniors and Freshmen will fall in line. They'll be marching right behind you. Stay in line and keep your faces forward until you reach the sidewalk," Mrs. Seaforth had admonished.

But how could you stay in line with someone tugging at your apron strings? Kathy looked around at Steve. He had a broad grin on his face. "I figured you'd march by my tree," he said. "Come on over here, I've got something to give you."

"Got to touch base first," she said, over her shoulder. "Stay where you are. I'll be back."

Conscientiously, she set one white shoe on the sidewalk and then raced back to the far side of the big oak. Steve swung around and looked at her proudly.

"Good-looking uniform," he said. "Good-looking girl inside."

He pulled a small leather camera case out of his pocket. Kathy's initials were in gold on the cover—all four of them.

"Katherine Nikola Elizabeth Martin, R.N.—I wanted the whole thing, but there wasn't room," he said.

"It's just beautiful, Steve."

"For taking pictures in the Big North," he explained.

"You really do want me to go to Alaska? Okay, if you say so. But I have to take State Board exams and a Red Cross blood-bank course before they'll take me. On the frontier, a nurse can't just step up to the mike and consult a doctor!"

"You'll manage," Steve said. He kept his eyes on the camera in Kathy's hands. "Open it," he said impatiently. "There's something inside."

Under the flap was a little pocket. Kathy caught sight

of a gleam of metal, felt with two fingers, and pulled out a small gold pin set with a tiny sapphire. If you looked closely, you could see that it was in the shape of a miniature fireman's badge.

"Nearest thing I have to a fraternity pin," Steve muttered, suddenly embarrassed to see Kathy blushing.

"I'll wear it over my heart," she said. "And Steve, if you look around you'll see that everybody's kissing everybody. It's—it's the proper thing at graduation."

sharon

clark